O.M.G

—— OH MY GODMOTHER ——

THE GLITTER TRAP

O.M.G

OH MY GODMOTHER

THE GLITTER TRAP

By Barbara Brauner
and James Iver Mattson

Illustrated by
Abigail Halpin

SCHOLASTIC INC.

ISBN 978-0-545-63343-7

12 11 10 9 8 7 6 5 4 3 2 1   14 15 16 17 18 19/0

Printed in the U.S.A.   40

First Scholastic printing, January 2014

Text is set in Fairfield Light.

O·M·G

OH MY GODMOTHER

THE GLITTER TRAP

PROLOGUE

* * * * *

My mom's name is Didi Unger, and that's a fine name.
My dad's name is Jonathan Ware, and that's a fine name, too.

My name is Lacey.

Lacey Unger-Ware.

Were they *crazy*?

How would you like to be "lacy underwear"?

I Googled it, and I can change my name when I turn eighteen. But that's six whole years away.

It'll be a miracle if I make it through middle school.

CHAPTER 1

My best friend, Sunny Varden, runs up to me before home-room. "You're not going to believe what's happened to Paige!"

"Let me guess," I say. "They're crowning her queen of sixth grade?"

"No!"

"She's getting her own TV show?"

"No!"

"The cute vampire in World Cultures is madly in love with her?"

Sunny stares at me, totally distracted: "Wait! There's a cute vampire in World Cultures? Is it Ian? He's so pale!"

"Sunny! How many times do I have to tell you? There are no vampires, no werewolves, no leprechauns. So, what's up with Paige?"

"You. Are. Not. Going. To. Believe. It!"

"Tell me, already!"

"Paige Harrington. The youngest head cheerleader in Lincoln Middle School history. Most popular girl in the universe . . . has a ZIT! A big red one. Right on her chin!"

No way! If anyone's gonna get big red zits, it's me, not Paige. She's so perfect that she went from New Girl to Most Popular in a single month. Nobody with zits could have done that.

Sunny drags me down the hall toward the gym. We turn the corner, and there's Paige, hanging a poster for Friday's football game. And sure enough, she's got a zit on her chin—it's *huge!* I pull out my cell phone to take a picture.

I'm not a bad person, really. I'm nice to old people and small animals. I never even kill bugs. But I *am* going to post this picture on Facebook, with a funny comment, because when Paige Harrington has a zit, the world needs to know.

Then, the big red dot on her chin catches the light and *sparkles.*

"That's not a zit," I say to Sunny, totally exasperated.

What Sunny thought was a pimple is actually a chunk of glitter off the stupid football poster. Glitter is something the cheerleaders go crazy over, and I don't get it. It's just tiny bits of shiny plastic. Why is that so appealing?

When Paige sees Sunny and me staring at her, I take a couple of steps back and bump into the wall. Paige shouts: "Underwear Girl! *NO!*"

Sunny whispers, "Oh my gosh! Paige Harrington knows your name!" Which would be true if my name were Underwear Girl. I shrink back some more, so embarrassed I feel like I'm glued to the wall.

Wait a minute, I *am* glued to the wall. My hair is all tangled up in the sticky, sloppy, glitter glue on Paige's football poster.

Paige jumps off her ladder and runs over like she's going to murder me with her staple gun. But instead of stapling me to death, she pulls me away from the poster.

Ow! I get yanked, but a lot of my hair stays behind. The glitter glue is now all over my hair, my shirt, my jeans, and my backpack—but especially my hair. It looks like Glinda the Good Witch vomited on me.

Sunny chirps, "I think we can fix it!" as she tries to pick glitter off my clothes and stick it back on the ruined poster.

But Paige just scowls. *"Go away."*

And when the queen of sixth grade tells you to go away, you do.

CHAPTER

2

After school, I sit in my parents' restaurant working on my essay for the Highland Park Zoo intern contest. Every year, the zoo picks one middle school kid to help at the petting zoo. It's a job a zillion kids want, so you have to write about why they should choose you.

And they *should* choose me. I already know I want to be a veterinarian. One time, my hermit crab had a cracked claw, and I fixed it with Krazy Glue. That should impress the zoo people.

But what if that's not enough? I try to think. It's hard to concentrate in a restaurant kitchen when the cook is shouting at the waitress, and she's shouting right back. Mom and Dad have amazing lung power.

Dad yells, "Push the asparagus!"

Mom yells, "Where's the pilaf?"

Dad yells, "Xander! Xander! Get in here!"

Mom yells, "He's late! Again!"

I cover my ears with my hair to block out some of the noise. Big mistake. Heavy chunks of glitter fall onto my notebook.

Darn it, I've shampooed my hair three times. And instead of washing out, the glitter glue just got stickier and grosser. When I'm done with my essay, I'm planning to write a letter to the people at Tru-Shampoo. They've solved split ends and flyaway hair, so now it's time to do something about glue.

I flick the glitter chunks away with a fingernail and try to concentrate.

"Look, Lacey! Look!" A five-year-old hand plops onto the page in front of me, fingers wiggling to show off new glitter nail polish. *Unbelievable!* Why does everyone have the glitter gene except me?

My little sister, Madison, looks at me with her big blue eyes. By the time Madison came along, my parents were better at having kids. Madison's like me—only, she's version 2.0. Her eyes are bluer, her hair is wavier, her name is simpler. I'm Lacey Unger-Ware; she's just Madison Ware. My parents had seven years to rethink the hyphen. But if they wanted to be fair, they should have at least named her Tupper.

Madison waves her glittery fingernails in front of my face again. "Don't you love them?"

"They're *gorgeous.*"

But Madison's too little to get sarcasm. "I know!" Then she

stares at my hair. "Sparkly!" She can't resist patting it. "Sticky, too!"

I am *so* going to write to Tru-Shampoo.

Madison pats my hair some more, trying to decide if sparkly beats sticky. Sparkly wins, and Madison beams. "You look like Sugarplum Barbie!" She raises her hands above her head and pirouettes around the table. She's so adorable I almost forget I'm annoyed with her.

Madison twirls around Mom, who is passing with a big tray of plates. I expect a crash, but Mom just smiles and does a little dance turn, getting out of the way.

Dad takes a break from whatever he's frying and does a little spin himself, finishing with a triple-flip spatula toss. Madison applauds, and he takes a silly half-bow.

I would never, ever, admit it to Mom and Dad, but it's nice here in the kitchen. It's warm, and the food smells good, and we're all together. One loud family.

"LACEY!" Dad shouts from across the room. I know what this means, so I look down and start writing really fast in my notebook.

"LACEY UNGER-WARE! I KNOW YOU CAN HEAR ME!"

Sure I can hear him. People in Canada can hear him! I crouch way down over my essay.

Dad plunks a couple of takeout boxes in front of me. I look up with a blank expression, like I've never seen a takeout box in my life.

Dad says, "Xander's late again."

"Uh-huh."

"The customer's only two blocks away. And they prepaid."

"Uh-huh."

"Be sure to wear the T-shirt."

"Dad! No!"

"It's good advertising for the restaurant."

"No!"

"Please! We're swamped. I really need you to pitch in."

I'm about to explain how this essay is going to affect my entire future. First, I'll be the zoo intern, then I'll get in to a good college, then I'll be a famous veterinarian who works with polar bears. Or maybe pandas. Or maybe some other kind of bear that I'll discover in the Amazon. And it all depends on this one life-or-death essay.

That argument would probably work with Dad, who may be loud but is a big softy underneath. But he looks so hopeful that I just can't bring myself to mention the bears and my future.

I pick up the boxes, sigh loudly, and head out the door.

"Don't forget the T-shirt!" Dad calls after me.

CHAPTER 3

It's dusk when I carry the takeout boxes out of the restaurant and check the delivery address: 1422 Eastlake Street.

I can't believe Dad made me wear this T-shirt. You're probably thinking, *How bad can it be?* First, it's lime green—you can see it from space. Some scientist guy in China is looking at his satellite feed right now and saying, "My eyes! My eyes! You're hurting my eyes!"

And what kind of crazy people name a restaurant the Hungry Moose? Right. My parents. The same ones who named me Lacey Unger-Ware.

Finally, there's the picture on the T-shirt. It's supposed to be a moose, but it looks more like a cross-eyed Great Dane. My mom drew it, and she's such a nice person that everybody pretended it was good. But it's not. I mean, really, *really* not.

I just hope I don't see anyone I know.

Eastlake Street has a lot of big houses where doctors and lawyers live. And you should see the lawns. *Green.* Just green. No dandelions or bleached-out dog-pee patches like in my neighborhood.

At house number 1422, there's a ginormous moth circling the porch light, and I wonder about this for a second. On a street this nice, you'd think there'd be a rule against bugs.

As I ring the doorbell, I'm thinking about how much I want to get back to the restaurant and take this T-shirt off. The door opens. . . .

Oh no.

Oh no!

OH NO!

It's Paige Harrington.

I can't help blushing. My burning red face must really clash with my lime-green T-shirt, because Paige stares at me as if I were a clown from planet Dork. Maybe I'll be lucky, and she won't recognize me. "Underwear Girl?" she says, surprised. I'm *never* lucky.

"Uh . . . hi!" I stammer. "I didn't know you lived here."

Paige can't take her eyes off my hair. "Is that glitter?"

"Uh . . . yes."

"Nice."

Unlike Madison, *I* do get sarcasm.

Paige grabs the boxes out of my hands and closes the door without another word.

I don't know how it's possible, but I blush even harder. I can't make up my mind if I'm more mad or humiliated. Maybe I'm madiliated.

As I bolt down the steps, there's a buzz of little wings. That stupid moth! It's decided that I'm more interesting than the porch light, and it circles around my head, making this weird, excited *GLURRR!* noise.

I wave it away with my hand, but it keeps dive-bombing my hair. *GLURRR! GLURRR! GLURRR!*

I hurry down the sidewalk, hoping that if I move away from the light, the moth will leave me alone. It doesn't. *GLURRR!*

I scurry up Eastlake Street. *GLURRR!*

I start to run. *GLURRRRR!* This moth just won't give up. I'm usually not scared of bugs, but this is spooky. I run even faster.

Suddenly, it's quiet. Yay! It's gone! Then . . .

GLURRRRRRRRR!!!!

I feel like I'm trapped in one of those scary movies my mom won't let me watch, where the sound is coming from . . .

. . . *inside the house!*

GGGGGGGLURRRRRRRRRRRRRR!

The moth is in my hair. Yuck!

I reach up to pull it out and then stop myself. Which is worse? A wiggling live moth or a squished and guts-oozing dead one?

A guts-oozing dead moth. No question.

CHAPTER 4

Ten minutes later, I stand in my bedroom holding up strand after strand of glittery, gluey hair. The moth is in there someplace; I can hear it *GLUURRRING.*

My big orange cat, Julius, crouches on the dresser, his butt shaking the way it does when he's about to pounce. Once, he attacked Madison's Ballerina Barbie, and Barbie lost a foot.

"Don't even think about it!" I say as I push him off the dresser. He stalks away, his feelings hurt.

Where's the moth? I keep searching. Wait, there it is! Ew! Ew! It's huge! I grab scissors to cut it out—and the moth SCREAMS.

And I scream, too, louder than I've ever screamed, maybe louder than anyone has ever screamed.

Because it's not a moth. *Moths don't have faces!*

I snip off the hair and the whatever-it-is falls to the floor.

Ew! It's squirming! It's horrible! But then I see a flash of brilliant color, like butterfly wings.

I crouch down to get a better look. Along with the wings and the face, I see a little dress made of shiny fabric. OMG! It's a little woman! Am I dreaming?

I reach out my hand to touch her—and she bites me, hard. OW! I am definitely not dreaming!

The tiny woman struggles to free her wings from the sticky glitter glue and my cut-off hair. But she doesn't look like you'd expect a fairy to look. Her face has too much makeup, her lipstick is smeary, and her red hair has white roots. In fact, she looks a lot like Dad's aunt Ginny after a hard week in Vegas.

"You're a monster!" she says in a raspy little voice. Wow! She even sounds like Aunt Ginny. I wonder if she's been trying to quit smoking for the past thirty years, too? My mouth drops open.

"And close your mouth. No one wants to look at that."

Some of the glitter in my hair catches the light, and she covers her eyes as if it's blinding her. "Glur! Cover it up! Cover it up!"

"My hair?"

"No. The glur! The shiny glur!"

I ask, "The glitter, you mean?"

"Yes! Glitter! Glur! Cover it up! *Cover it up!*"

I stuff my hair under a baseball cap as the little woman peers out from between her fingers. She says, "You're a very bad girl. Setting a glitter trap!"

"A glitter trap?"

"Don't play innocent with me. All that glur and glue! It's a glitter trap! What else could it be?"

What is her problem? "You think I did this to my hair on purpose?" I say. "It's not my fault that Paige Harrington is a glitter maniac!"

The little woman's eyes open wide. "Oh, dear lord. Paige Harrington! I'm supposed to be with her right now!" She pulls at the sticky hair. "Get me loose! Get me loose!"

"What are you, exactly?"

"I'm a fairy godmother, you ninny! Isn't that obvious? Help me! GET ME LOOSE!"

Now I'm getting mad. "No!"

"Don't make me hurt you!"

"You're the size of my finger! How are you going to hurt me?"

"With this magic wand. You're going to be sorry you ever met Katarina Sycorax!" She reaches into her sleeve, pulls out a pin-size wand, and aims it at herself: "Hair that binds now unwinds!" The tip of the wand glows brightly, and the hair that's stuck to her dissolves into a million pieces.

Then she fixes me with her beady little eyes and says, "Your turn."

There's a moment when time freezes. I know she's only three inches tall, but she's really mad, and she's got a magic wand, and I don't want to dissolve into a million pieces. I hold up my hands and say, "Don't shoot! Don't zap! Uh . . . don't wand!"

She chants, "Girl who annoyed me, shall now a flea be!"

Oh no. Oh no! OH NO! I don't want to be a flea! The tip of the wand glows again, even brighter than before. But just as she swings it . . .

. . . Julius pounces and swallows her up in one gulp. He sits there with a smug expression on his face, as if a fairy is the best cat treat ever.

OMG! *He ate her!* What am I going to do?

Then I hear the sound of the front door opening, and Mom calls, "Lacey? Are you here?"

I pick up Julius. "Spit her out!"

Julius clamps his mouth shut, so I use my fingers to pry it open. I see his sharp teeth and rough pink tongue, but no little woman with butterfly wings. Sure, she wasn't sweet and kind like fairies are supposed to be, but that didn't mean I wanted her to get eaten by a cat.

Mom walks into my bedroom with Madison right behind her. Mom says, "There you are! Why didn't you come back to the restaurant?"

I blurt out the truth: "I got this moth caught in my hair. Only, it wasn't a moth, it was a fairy godmother!"

Madison loves this idea. Her eyes light up, and her lips form into a round *ooh* shape. "It *was*?"

Mom just nods her head. "Right, Lacey."

"No, really!"

"And where is this fairy godmother now?"

"Julius ate her!"

Mom nods again. I admit it—I wouldn't believe me, either.

Madison pulls Julius out of my arms and tells him, "Bad kitty!" She cuddles him and then looks confused. With her ear at Julius's stomach, she says, "Mommy! I hear bad words!"

I grab Julius back and listen to his stomach, too. Yep. Very bad words. I would tell you what they are, but I don't have enough money to put in my mom's swear jar. Believe me, there are about a thousand dollars' worth of curse words coming from inside him.

I expect Mom to start asking all sorts of questions. Instead, she acts like a grown-up and doesn't see what's right in front of her face. "Madison! It's bath time! Lacey, you stay here in your room. When you want to tell me the truth about where you were, you can come out." She leads Madison out of the room and shuts my door.

I pull Julius's mouth open again and talk into it: "Are you all right in there?"

Katarina's voice booms out, moist and echoey like it's coming from the bottom of a well: "NO! Get me out of this creature!"

"I can't!"

"I'm halfway to the small intestine. GET ME OUT!"

Julius scrambles out of my arms and darts under the bed. I crouch down and reach for him, but he squirms away from my fingers into the farthest back corner.

Suddenly I remember this time at the restaurant when a guy was choking on a meatball and my dad did the Heimlich maneuver on him. It's simple—if someone's choking, you grab them around the stomach from behind and push up hard.

It might work. Anyway, I don't have any other ideas. I lunge for Julius and drag him out by his left hind leg. "I'm really, really sorry," I say, and then I squeeze the heck out of him.

PTUI! Katarina flies across the room like a chunk of meatball and hits the wall.

I can't believe it worked! When I'm a famous veterinarian, I'm going to have to tell the whole world about the Heimlich maneuver for cats.

Julius struggles in my arms, so I pet him and say, "I'm really, really, *really* sorry!"

A voice comes from across the room: "Don't worry about that furbag! What about me?"

Julius and I both look toward Katarina. He's already forgotten how it worked out the last time, and he tries to get down and eat her again. Cats never learn, but I do. I open my bedroom door a crack and drop him outside in the hall.

Katarina looks like something the cat threw up. (Because

she is.) Squashed wings, slimy clothes, and hair covered with chunks of half-digested cat food. "Don't just stand there! Clean me off!"

She's so gross I don't want to touch her, but she's very loud and very bossy. "I said, clean me off now! Pick me up!"

I try not to shudder as Katarina climbs onto my hand, making tiny slimy footprints on my palm.

CHAPTER

5

It doesn't take long to fill the bathroom sink with warm water and strawberry-scented bubbles.

Katarina smiles for the first time. "Oooh! Bubbles!" She eases herself into the water, still fully dressed. Which I'm glad about—I was afraid she was going to order me to find her a tiny washer-dryer.

As she relaxes in the foam, I finally have time to think about what's been happening: I've just caught a fairy! Weird, but also kind of cool, even if she was mean to me. Maybe the worst is over, and Katarina and I are going to be friends.

Nope. Her smile turns into a frown and she glares at me, so not-friendly it's ridiculous.

I sigh. "What's wrong now?"

"What do you think? I just got eaten by a cat and every bone in my body hurts! They're all probably broken! I know my wings

are!" She splashes the bubbles away. "And I hate strawberries! I only like essence of lilac!"

"We don't have any essence of lilac."

In a snarky voice that would make Paige Harrington proud, she says, "Of course you don't. In a household like this? I'll make it myself."

She reaches into her sleeve and then gets a horrified look on her face. "Oh no!"

"What's wrong?"

"Where's my wand! I need my wand!"

What if it's still inside Julius? Maybe it'll come out the other end, but I'm not going to dig through his litter box to find out. I don't want to say this to Katarina, so I copy the low, soothing voice Mom uses on Dad when he's lost the remote control again: "All right, all right. We'll find it." I sound so much like Mom it's amazing. Maybe I could be an actress.

Then a faint *bleep! bleep!* comes from my bedroom.

"What's that sound?" I ask.

Katarina looks at me like I'm the stupidest girl in the world. "Wand alarm. Go fetch it!" She presses a jewel on her dress, making more *bleep* sounds.

I go into my bedroom, but there's no sign of the wand.

"I don't see it," I yell.

Bleep! Bleep! The sounds come again. "I still don't see it!"

BLEEP! BLEEP! BLEEP! BLEEP! BLEEP!

I say, "You can *bleep* all you want. I *still* don't see it!"

"Don't see what?" Mom says from the bathroom. Uh-oh. She must have gone in through Madison's door.

I hurry into the bathroom and find Mom turning on the water in the tub while Madison stands on tiptoe so she can peer into the sink. "Oooh, bubbles!" she says, sounding exactly like Katarina.

"Don't see what?" Mom asks me again.

Madison starts poking around in the bubbles, and there's a flash of butterfly wing beneath the foam. I've got to do something.

"Oh *there* it is!" I reach into the sink and grab Katarina, covering her up with my hand. "I've been looking everyplace for my butterfly hair clip. And now I remember I was washing it."

Madison gives me a funny look. "You don't have a butterfly hair clip."

"I do, too! Sunny gave it to me, and it got dirty, so I washed it." Then I tell Mom, "Well, I'd better go stay in my room like I'm supposed to."

Mom looks at me suspiciously. Maybe I *couldn't* be an actress.

CHAPTER

6

"Put me down this instant, before I bite you again," Katarina says once we're safe in my bedroom.

"But you're dripping," I say, blotting her with the bottom of my Hungry Moose T-shirt.

"Ow! Don't be so rough!" Then she takes a closer look at the green fabric. "What an ugly color!"

"I know!"

I put her down on top of my dresser, and she frowns when she sees herself in the mirror. "Just look at me! I made it through the Great Fire of London without a smudge of soot! I was on the *Titanic* and I didn't even get wet! I helped that girl win *Survivor*, and my wings looked fabulous the whole time!" She stamps her feet in fury. "This is all your fault. You and your glitter trap!"

"Not so loud! Mom will hear us!" I turn on my TV to cover the sound of our voices.

Katarina pokes at her tattered wings. "You're just lucky I didn't spontaneously cocoon when your beast attacked me!"

"Cocoon? Like a butterfly?"

She ignores my question as she tries to tug her wings into shape. "This is ridiculous! I need my wand!" She pushes the jewel on her dress again. *Bleep! Bleep!*

We both look at the floor. She points. "There!"

"Where?"

"There!"

I finally see the pin-size wand sticking out of the carpet. When I pick it up, a small, sharp zap shoots through me, the kind of electric jolt you get when you touch a doorknob after you've rubbed your feet on the carpet.

"Give me that!" Katarina snatches the wand out of my fingers and chants: "Do your duty! Bring back my beauty!"

I'm thinking she wasn't all that beautiful even before Julius ate her, but I'm smart enough not to say this out loud.

Katarina starts to raise her wand above her head, then grimaces. "Ow! My arm!" She lowers her arm and tries chanting it again, "Do your duty! Bring back my beauty!" Her arm barely moves. *"OW!"*

She grabs her right elbow with her left hand and chants one more time, her voice high-pitched and scared: "Do your duty! Bring back my beauty!" She shoves her elbow up as hard as she can and then SHRIEKS in pain. Katarina drops the wand, and I have to catch it before it gets lost in the carpet again.

To try to make Katarina feel better, I use my soothing Mom voice again. "It looks like you sprained your shoulder. That happened to my dad once playing basketball. He was fine in a couple of weeks."

"Weeks!" Katarina wails. "That will be too late! The full moon will have come and gone!" She puts her head in her hands and sobs like the world is ending. Not just the world—the galaxy and the universe, too.

"Don't cry! It can't be that bad!"

She looks at me, tears streaming down her face. "Can't be that bad! *Can't be that bad!*" Then she wails even louder.

"You've got to be quiet! Please!"

Katarina takes a couple of deep breaths, trying to pull herself together. "Well, I hope you're happy! You ruined my life. You ruined Paige Harrington's life. And you ruined your life."

"What are you talking about?"

"You don't have any idea of the cosmic forces you've unleashed! You and your glitter trap."

"That was an accident!"

"It doesn't matter?! Let me spell it out for you. I'm a fairy godmother. I was sent to help Paige Harrington get her dream. Follow me so far?"

I sigh, but she repeats, "Do you follow me so far? Answer me!"

"Yes, I'm following you."

"You stopped me from helping Paige by trapping me in your hair. That was bad enough, but I could have recovered from that. *Then* you allowed your cat to maim me!" To demonstrate the "maim" part, she raises her arm a little and winces.

Wow, she's really rubbing this stuff in. Plus, you don't "allow" cats to do anything—they do exactly what they want. I just say, "I'm sorry you're hurt. You can stay here in my room till you get better."

"I won't be better for weeks. Therefore, Paige won't get her dream by the night of the full moon, and I will have failed. And when I fail, I will be demoted. Possibly to tooth fairy. But most probably to dryer fairy." Katarina shudders at the thought.

"What's a dryer fairy?"

"Where do you think all those socks go? Dryer fairies. It's an endless cycle of sock stealing and lint. And I'm allergic to lint."

"What did they do before there were dryers?"

"Clothesline fairies. At least then, you had sunshine and fresh air. Now it's all basements and fabric softener."

"That does sound pretty bad."

"Bad for me—worse for you."

I'm starting to freak out. "I'm going to be a dryer fairy?"

Katarina, her old crankiness returning, says, "Of course not! Will you please let me finish?" She stares at me to make sure I'm not going to say anything else, and then continues. "Because you stopped Paige from getting her dream . . . none of *your* dreams will come true. Not for the rest of your life."

I've never heard of anything so unfair! Paige was the one who put too much glitter on the poster and messed up my hair. And if she hadn't ordered takeout, I wouldn't even have been at her house!

Katarina seems happy about how mad I look. "Karma sucks," she says.

"What are we going to do about it?"

"There's nothing *to* do. We're doomed."

"There must be something!"

"There's nothing. And now if you don't mind, I'm very tired, and I'm going to bed."

She opens the lid of my jewelry box and climbs in, tossing out my bracelets and rings, which land on the dresser with a clatter. I can't believe she's going to bed when we're doomed!

I say, "But we need to talk about this!"

"No, we don't. Good night!"

Click! She closes the jewelry box and vanishes from sight. I feel like shaking it or throwing it out the window.

Or maybe I'll just curl up in a ball on the floor and cry.

CHAPTER 7

"What's wrong with you?" Sunny asks in homeroom the next morning. I guess she's noticed the black circles under my eyes.

You're probably thinking I was up all night worrying about the whole dreams-not-coming-true-for-the-rest-of-my-life thing. That's not it at all. I couldn't sleep because Katarina was snoring. I mean, SNORING! I thought fairies were supposed to be dainty and ladylike. Geez!

The snoring was so bad that Julius wouldn't even sleep on my bed, where he's slept ever since I brought him home from the animal shelter when he was eight weeks old.

Sunny has probably also noticed that I'm typing away on the class computer instead of gossiping with her like I usually do. But that's because my essay for the zoo intern contest has to be e-mailed by noon. I was going to finish it last night, but I had fairy problems.

Sunny repeats, "Lacey! What's wrong with you?"

I'm tempted to tell her the whole story, but between you and me, Sunny's not good in a crisis. Last year, her pants split at recess, and she got so upset she had to go home. That happened to me once, and I covered it with my sweater like a normal person. So I don't know how Sunny would react if she found out I had accidentally trapped a fairy godmother in my hair and would never have a dream come true.

Besides . . . maybe Katarina is wrong. Maybe she's making the whole thing up to give me a hard time, just like she did this morning when she wouldn't come out of the jewelry box even when I brought her two blueberries and a Frosted Mini-Wheat for breakfast.

So I look Sunny straight in the eyes and say, "Nothing is wrong! I'm just working on my zoo essay."

"Oh, right. Want me to help check the spelling?"

"You're a terrible speller."

"I am not."

"Okay—I'm writing about getting a baby giraffe for the petting zoo. Spell *giraffe*."

Sunny looks at me like I just stabbed her in the heart. She says, "Never mind! I only wanted to help."

I feel bad, but I tell myself that Sunny will get over it. So I keep working until I finally type *And that's why, if you choose me, I will make a wonderful zoo intern.*

The bell rings right as I hit send. Smiling for the first time today, I look up to tell Sunny I'm done. But she's already gone.

In science class, I listen to Mr. Carver talking about Pluto and how it's not officially a planet anymore. Most days, this would be interesting, but today I've got bigger things on my mind than a chunk of rock.

The classroom door opens, and Paige walks in. "You're late," Mr. Carver says.

She hands him a hall pass and says, "Principal Nazarino said it was okay. I was working on an emergency football poster. Somebody wrecked the last one I did." She gives me a dirty look, and I shrink down in my chair.

Mr. Carver frowns. "Your education is more important than a football poster."

"Yeah, if you're a total geek," Paige says under her breath. When the popular kids snicker, she gets a funny expression on her face. If it were anyone except Paige, I'd say she looks like she feels a tiny bit bad. But she's probably just wishing she had said something even meaner.

CHAPTER

8

At lunchtime, Sunny is waiting for me at our usual table in the courtyard. "Hey, Lacey! Heard from the zoo people yet?"

"If they like my essay, they'll call me in for an interview. But that won't be till next week, at the earliest."

I'm happy she's even talking to me. They don't call her Sunny for nothing—she just can't stay mad very long. As I sit down, I put a cookie on her tray. "This is for you. I didn't mean it about the spelling."

"But chocolate chip is your favorite, too!" Sunny hands me half, and I eat it in one bite. She just nibbles hers. She can make a cookie last longer than anyone I know. Then she says, "G—I—R—A—F—F—E. Giraffe."

"I knew you could spell it."

"I looked it up in English class. Why does it start with a G and not a J?"

"Good question."

Then Sunny asks, "Did you know that people used to call giraffes camelopards, because they thought they looked like camels with leopard spots?"

"No. That's cool," I say, picturing a camel with spots on its hump.

Sunny reaches the last chunk of cookie. "This is for Seymour."

Peering up in the tree above us, I wonder where he is. Seymour is an almost-tame squirrel that we feed every day at lunch. He's really smart and brave—and usually jumps on the table as soon as we sit down. But he's not jumping on the table today. We both start calling, "Seymour! Seymour!"

Sunny points. "There he is!" He's in the highest branches of the tree, looking down at us with his little black eyes.

I hold up the chunk of cookie. "Come on, Seymour! It's chocolate chip!"

But he just chatters at me angrily. It's the same sound he makes when he tries to scare away crows.

"What's the matter with you?" I say.

He chatters a little more, and then he disappears into the branches.

I turn to Sunny, worried. "Maybe some of the eighth-grade kids were teasing him."

"I know what's wrong with him! He's gone . . . squirrelly!" Sunny laughs at her own bad joke, and I can't help laughing, too. I'm sure Seymour will be fine tomorrow.

As Sunny and I finish our lunches, we hear the faint sound of a piano. Sunny cocks her head. "Are those the auditions? Finally!"

I listen, too. Our music teacher, Mr. Griffith, has written a rock-opera version of "Cinderella" that is going to be this fall's school play. He was supposed to finish it six weeks ago, but he kept telling us that musical genius can't be rushed. Maybe genius can't be rushed, but now the play's going to be. No matter what, the audience is showing up a week from Saturday. The school has been sending out e-mails for months, and the posters are up all over town.

The song being played on the piano *is* pretty catchy. Not

genius level, but hummable. Sunny and I get up and look through the open music-room window.

Mr. Griffith sits at the piano, playing with his eyes closed. I guess he's showing everybody he's so good that he doesn't even have to look at the keys.

There must be about twenty kids in the room listening to him. Mainly girls, but some boys, too, including Scott Dearden, the cutest boy in middle school. He has longer eyelashes than anyone I know.

Sunny whispers, "I guess we know who's going to be Prince Charming." After I nod in agreement, she asks, "Who do you think is going to be Cinderella?"

"Well, we know it's not going to be me."

"You could totally be Cinderella! You have a great voice!"

"Me perform in front of people? No way! I'd barf!"

"No, you wouldn't!" Sunny thinks about it for a moment. "Oh, yeah. You would. The Girl Scout Fun-Time Sing Out . . ."

". . . where I had a solo. And instead of singing, I threw up beanie weenies all over the first three rows of the audience. Including your mom. She never forgave me."

"She forgave you. But she still can't look at beanie weenies."

Sunny and I probably shouldn't be standing here spying like this, but it's too good to miss. It's like a reality show being put on just for the two of us. We scan the crowd of hopeful girls. Most of them have come to the audition wearing some sort of costume. Three girls stand off to the side holding "magic wands": a drumstick, a chrome baton with streamers on the end, and a plastic *Star Wars* Lightsaber. Sunny says, "Those have got to be fairy godmothers."

I wish I could tell Sunny that a real fairy godmother has smeary lipstick and a bad attitude. Instead, I point at the girl with the drumstick. "Chloe Martin's gonna get the part for sure."

"Her wand looks stupid."

"But she does an excellent British accent. She's watched *Mary Poppins* over eighty times."

Sunny half agrees with me. "Yeah. But they're going to have to get her a better wand."

The rest of the girls are all wannabe Cinderellas. Some of them are the "before" version. One girl wears an apron. Another has artistically placed smudges on her face. A third is barefoot and carries a broom for cinder sweeping.

Then there are the "after" Cinderellas. (Let's face it, this is where the fun is.) One girl has a puffy hoop skirt that everyone keeps stepping on. Three girls wear tiaras. And seven girls are missing a shoe.

But before or after, these girls are giving it their all. Every one of them is desperate to stand out.

Then Paige walks in, late as usual, and the hopeful expressions vanish from every face. Paige doesn't have a costume, hasn't done a single thing special. She's just Paige. But it's like she has an invisible spotlight shining on her.

I have to wonder: why does a girl with an invisible spotlight need a fairy godmother? Paige is already beautiful, popular, and a cheerleader. And now she's going to get the lead in the school play just by showing up. It's so unfair. I'm doomed, Katarina's doomed, and Paige is going to be Cinderella without even trying.

Mr. Griffith finally stops tinkling away on the piano and opens his eyes. He says, "So that was the music for Cinderella's big solo after she leaves the ball. It's called, 'I Lost My Shoe and You!' It's the character's big moment, and, frankly, it's the moment that will make one of you into a star. If there's a Hollywood talent scout in the crowd, you'll be snapped up and on your way to international fame."

Mr. Griffith is *insane*. The only way a Hollywood talent scout would come to our town would be if he accidentally fell out of one of the jets that cross overhead on their way to L.A.

But then I look at Paige again. With her luck, this is exactly what's going to happen. One song, and she'll go from queen of the school to movie star.

Mr. Griffith stands up and passes out the sheet music. The other girls study the lyrics nervously, but Paige just gives them one quick glance. For her, this is so easy.

"Let's get started, shall we? Who's first?"

The rest of the girls look hopeful, but Mr. Griffith says, "Paige, why don't you break the ice? Come stand by the piano and show us what you've got."

Paige glides over confidently, and Mr. Griffith plays the first few notes of the song. She opens her mouth and sings: *"I lost my shoe and you! I can't believe it's true!"*

Every single person in the room stares at her in astonishment.

And it's not because of how perfect she sounds. Paige sounds . . .

. . . *bad.*

Bad like fingernails on chalkboards. Bad like screeching cats. Bad like . . . *bad!*

Sunny and I look at each other in disbelief. This can't be right.

Mr. Griffith stares at Paige, as shocked as everybody else. "Wrong key, Paige. My fault entirely." He hits a note on the piano. "Let's try it again, a little lower."

Paige studies the sheet music, and there's a tiny bit of doubt on her face. But she straightens her shoulders and nods to Mr. Griffith that she's ready. She sings again: *"I lost my shoe and you! I can't believe it's true!"*

I don't know how it's possible, but she's even worse than before. The other kids laugh and cover their ears. One boy even clasps his hands together and trills in a high squeal, *"I can't believe it's true! No one sings worse than you!"*

Everyone guffaws. And it's sad, but he actually sounds a lot better than Paige did.

Paige looks over and sees even Scott Dearden, who is usually as nice as he is cute, trying to hide a grin.

Mr. Griffith tries to calm everyone down. "Quiet, everybody! This project is about exploration. It was very brave of Paige to put herself on the line like this." He turns to Paige again. "Have you thought about trying out for one of the dancing mice? They don't sing. They squeak."

The kids all make high-pitched squeaking sounds and laugh even louder.

Trying to keep some of her popular-girl dignity, Paige pretends she's above it all and looks out the window—where Sunny and I stand gawking at her. And we *are* gawking. You would be, too.

But seeing us is the last straw for Paige. She's had enough. She bursts into tears and runs out of the room.

The other kids can't stop laughing. In school, it's always kind of exciting to see one of the popular crowd take a fall. This might sound odd coming from a girl who was going to post Paige's zit on Facebook, but I feel kind of bad. Paige put herself on the line and got shot down. Me, I expect to be shot down. Most of us get used to it. But I don't think it's ever happened to Paige Harrington before.

I think I've just discovered why Paige needs a fairy godmother.

CHAPTER

9

On Thursdays, Sunny has karate class, so I walk home from school alone. Walking home from school is usually my favorite part of the day, but now I can't stop thinking about what happened to Paige. Katarina would say that what happened at the audition was all my fault, but I'm not the fairy godmother, Katarina is. According to her, I'm just a glitter-trapping monster.

I pass the house where Mr. Anderson and his dog, Barnaby, live. Barnaby is a sleepy old basset hound who's almost too lazy to move, but he always gets off the porch and walks up to the white picket fence so I can scratch his ears. He's a sweetie. But today . . .

ROWF! ROWF! ROWF!

Barnaby lunges at me from behind the fence, like I really *am* a monster.

"Barnaby! What's wrong with you?"

ROWF! ROWF! ROWF!

He keeps barking and growling so much that I'm worried he's going to drop dead from a heart attack. So I walk away, but can't help wondering what's up with him. Maybe he ate some bad Alpo.

When I walk past the little park near my house, Mrs. Garcetti is sitting on one of the benches throwing bread crumbs to the pigeons like she always does. The pigeons love her. "Hi, Lacey!" she calls.

"Hi, Mrs. Garcetti!" I call back.

There's a big flock of happy, cooing pigeons around her. But when I walk past on the sidewalk, they get quiet all at once.

Thirty-four pigeons turn and stare at me.

This is weird. The pigeons seem kind of mad, as if I'd been saying mean things about them behind their backs.

"Come on, babies. Aren't you hungry? Eat for Mama." Mrs. Garcetti throws another big handful of bread crumbs, but the birds don't even notice.

They can't take their eyes off me. And I can't take my eyes off them. I take a step sideways . . .

. . . and so do all the pigeons.

I take another step . . .

. . . and so do they.

I lift one foot . . .

. . . and all the pigeons lift one foot.

Okay. This is officially creepy.

I take off running, as fast as I can.

I want to warn you that this next part is really gross. And if you've got a weak stomach, you should skip ahead to Chapter 10 right now. I'll give you till the count of three.

One.

Two.

Two and a half.

Three.

Still here? Don't say I didn't warn you. I even gave you a "half," which I didn't have to do.

I run with all my might toward my house. And the pigeons near Mrs. Garcetti fly up with a big whoosh of wings and follow me.

Suddenly, dozens of pigeons are in the air right over my head, with more arriving every second. If you were standing across the street, it would look like I was running under a big, dark rain cloud.

Rain clouds. And flocks of pigeons . . . Well, there's no nice way to say this. Flocks of pigeons . . . poop.

Splat! A big, wet, white plop of pigeon poop lands on the sidewalk right next to me. Splat! There's another plop. Then another. Then another. I keep running.

EWWWWWWWW! Pigeon poop hits my shoulder.

There's a covered bus shelter down the street. For once in

my life, I run faster than any of the kids on the track team and make it under the clear plastic roof just in time.

Ker-splat! Ker-splat times a thousand! Pigeon poop showers down on the bus shelter in buckets.

This is so gross! Unbelievably gross! And I have pigeon poop on my favorite sweater. Ew. Ew. Ew. Ew.

The poopstorm seems to be slowing down, and I think the worst is over. But then hundreds more pigeons fly in from every direction, just like somebody texted them to come join the fun. I've got to get out of here. But how?

There must be something I can use as a pigeon-poop umbrella. The bench is bolted down, so that won't work. The garbage can is one of those open-lid kinds, so that won't work. But someone has taped a big poster-board yard-sale sign on the back wall of the bus shelter. It's pretty flimsy, but it's all I have. I put the yard-sale poster over my head—and RUN.

The gigantic flock of pigeons follows me all the way to my house. But the yard-sale sign works great. A few more steps and I'll be safe inside the front door, and pigeon-free.

Uh-oh. To turn the front doorknob, I'm going to have to use my hand, which means putting down the sign, which means . . .

. . . the pigeons will get me for sure. *Poopageddon!*

Kicking the door with my foot, I shout, "Let me in! LET ME IN!" But no one comes to my rescue, since no one's home. *Duh.* But your brain wouldn't be working correctly right now, either.

Maybe I can get in the back door. I sure can't wait around on the front steps all day with a gazillion crazy birds.

I sprint around to the side of the house and skid to a stop. There's a big maple tree in the backyard, and every square inch of it is covered with pigeons. And every one of them is waiting for me. The maple tree has so many birds on it that it's not green, it's pigeon-feather gray. There's no way I'm going under that tree.

But I don't have to. With an amazingly loud *FRRIIIPPP!* of fluttering wings, every pigeon on the tree takes flight and heads straight for me.

And there are just as many pigeons coming at me from the other direction. I'm trapped! I don't know if pigeons eat people, but these look like they might.

I spin sideways. There's a high fence blocking my way. On the other side, the wall of the house blocks me.

FRRRRIIIIIPPPPPP! The fluttering pigeons almost reach me. I look to my left: Madison's bedroom window is closed tight. I look to my right: there's my window. *And it's open!* I drop the poster board and grab the windowsill.

Bird wings engulf me as I desperately hoist myself inside the window and slam it shut. Then, as quickly as they arrived, the pigeons fly off in a million directions.

Except for the white trail of bird poop leading to my window, it's as if the pigeons were never there.

CHAPTER

10

After the window dive into my bedroom, it takes me a while to catch my breath. I'm about to wipe my sweaty forehead with my sleeve when I see that it's covered with poop. Ew! My sweater goes straight into the trash.

Then I hear a crunch . . . crunch . . . crunch sound.

OH NO! There's a pigeon in the room!

But the crunch sound isn't coming from a pigeon, it's coming from Katarina, who sits on my dresser calmly chewing on the Frosted Mini-Wheat I left her. (It's almost as big as her head.) She looks at me with fake sympathy. "Had a hard day, dear?"

"Yes, I had a hard day! Pigeons chased me!"

"Interesting. Anything else out of the ordinary?"

"What more do you want?" But then I think a moment. "Barnaby barked at me. And Seymour wouldn't come out of his tree. What's happening?"

"Isn't it obvious? It's your dream not coming true."

"What?"

Katarina talks very loudly and slowly—exactly the way my grandma speaks to people with accents, like she's going to make them understand through sheer lung power: "IT'S. YOUR. DREAM. NOT. COMING. TRUE!"

"I'm not talking about my dream! I'm talking about pigeons! What does my dream have to do with pigeons? Or Barnaby? Or Seymour?"

"Think about it. They're all animals, and they all hate you. You're going to have a little trouble being a zoo intern if every animal in the world despises you on sight."

"How did you know I wanted to be a zoo intern?" I ask, getting scared. *"Can you read minds?"*

"No, I read your essay. There was a copy in the trash can."

My knees suddenly feel weak, so I sit on the bed. Animals hate me? This is awful! "There's gotta be a way we can fix this!"

"That's exactly what Marie Antoinette said to my cousin Maude just before . . ." Katarina makes a slashing motion across her neck. "Maude lost her wings and got demoted to wood fairy."

"She lives in the woods?"

"No. She chops it. Night and day. Day and night. Chop, chop, chop."

"But if animals hate me, I won't ever get to be a veterinarian, either!"

Katarina just yawns and crawls into the jewelry box. "Right! Paige won't get her dream, and you won't get yours. 'We'll all live unhappily ever after. The end.'" She starts to pull the lid over her, but I hold it open. Katarina covers her face with her hands and pretends to snore. "Sleeping here. Go away."

I'm so annoyed that I turn the jewelry box upside down and shake her out. Katarina lands on the dresser with an angry yelp. "Now you've done it!" She pulls out her wand and shouts, "Boils and sores! Oozing pores!"

Yikes!

Katarina starts to raise her wand, but her injured shoulder makes her bend over in pain. "Ow!" The wand drops to the dresser, and I pick it up, thinking.

"Give me that!" she says.

I ignore her. There's nothing very complicated about this, it's really just a little stick. Suddenly, an amazing idea comes to me—an idea that could fix everything! I shout, "*I'll* be Paige's fairy godmother!"

Katarina snorts and grabs for the wand, but I keep it out of her reach.

I say, "Think about it! Paige's life is practically perfect already. I know what her wish is. She wants the lead part in the school play. I'll use the magic wand to fix her voice and get her the part. Voilà! Her dream comes true, and all our problems are solved."

"You have no idea what you're talking about! I had over a

century of training at the Academy before I was assigned my first case! You can't be a fairy godmother!"

"Sure I can!" I start waving the little wand around. Then I wave it some more. And a little more. "Nothing's happening."

"Of course it's not. Give me that."

I think about how Katarina uses the wand. Or used it, when her wand arm was still working. I point the wand at my unmade bed and say, "Make the bed." Nothing happens.

Katarina rolls her eyes. "Told you so. You're not godmother material."

I lower the wand and chew my lip, thinking some more. Maybe it's got to rhyme. Aiming the wand at my bedspread, I chant, "Bed's a disgrace! Put it in place!" One corner twitches a tiny bit, but you wouldn't even notice it if you weren't looking for it. And that's all that happens.

Katarina says, "I can't believe it!"

"You don't have to be sarcastic. I know it was pathetic."

"It wasn't pathetic, it was magic. Only one girl in a million has any magic in her at all."

For a second I still think she's making fun of me, but she actually does seem impressed. I'm one in a million? My dad always says that, but he's just being my dad.

Katarina looks at me thoughtfully. "There's a teeny tiny little chance your scheme might work. Maybe you *could* be Paige's fairy godmother and get us out of this mess."

"I can do it! I know I can!"

Katarina's still thoughtful. "No, it's impossible."

"Don't say that! It's possible! I, Lacey Unger-Ware, will be Paige Harrington's fairy godmother. No matter how hard it is, no matter what it takes. But I can't do it unless you help me."

"Won't work. You're too headstrong to teach."

"No, I'm not!"

"You don't listen."

"From now on, I'll listen to every single word you say."

Twenty minutes later, I'm still listening. Actually, that's not true. I stopped listening about ten minutes ago. Katarina is droning on and on about how being a fairy godmother is 99 percent about using the wand. I hear about the tradition of the wand, blah blah blah. The responsibility of the wand, blah blah blah. The style, skill, finesse, accuracy, blah blah blah blah blah. She's talking about a magic wand. And she's sucking every bit of magic out of it.

Who needs training? I made the bedspread move, right? I decide to stop the blah-blah-blahing and show Katarina that I'm a natural at this.

Looking around the room, I try to figure out what to zap. There's a row of stuffed animals on my bookshelf; at the end there's a cute plush shark that my dad brought me from a restaurant convention in Miami. I raise the wand.

Katarina glares at me. "What are you doing? Don't—"

I say in a loud, firm voice: "Shark from the reef, please chomp your teeth!"

And I point the wand right at the stuffed shark. Chomp! It makes a biting motion with its teeth. Just once, but that's all I need to prove that I'm gonna be good at this. "See! It's easy!"

"Do you have any idea of the forces you're meddling with, missy? It worked this time, but that shark could have . . ."

She doesn't finish her sentence, because the toy shark starts chomping its teeth like crazy. It bites the stuffed elephant. It bites the stuffed tiger. It bites my old teddy bear. There hasn't been this much biting since carnivore night on the Discovery Channel. Luckily, the shark's teeth are as fluffy and plush as the rest of it. So all it does to the other animals is plump them up like pillows.

"How do I make it stop, Katarina?"

"You can't."

The shark wriggles around so much that it falls off the shelf onto my bed. *CHOMP! CHOMP! CHOMP!* It attacks my bedspread.

"It's going to do that forever?"

"No, just until midnight. That's how long fairy-godmother spells last. Don't they teach you anything in school?"

"I must have been absent that day." I lean down closer to the shark to get a better look.

"Careful!"

Too late. The shark lunges off the bed and bites my ear as hard as it can with its soft teeth and strong jaws. I try to pull it off, but I can't budge it. "Do something!" I say to Katarina.

"Midnight, remember?"

With one sharp yank on its tail, I finally pull it free. It sits on the floor looking at me with its beady little eyes. Maybe I've tired it out.

Nope. The shark wriggles and flops out of sight under the bed. *Not* being able to see it is somehow a lot scarier than seeing it.

Maybe it's getting ready to jump out and bite me. Maybe . . . I suddenly feel a sharp poke on my leg. I can't help it, I SCREAM.

I turn around—and it's Madison, who SCREAMS, too. (Madison screams louder than anyone I know.) Katarina puts her hands over her ears and hides behind a lamp.

Mom comes in from the hallway, not looking too concerned. "Why all the screaming?"

Madison says, "I screamed because Lacey screamed." And they both stare at me.

"Madison poked me."

"Madison, stop poking your sister. And Lacey, stop scream-ing. Now, get your things. Dad's waiting for us at the restaurant. Lacey, where's your sweater?"

Mom doesn't need to know that the sleeves got pooped on by a million pigeons, so I say, "I forgot it at school."

"Well, get your jacket, and let's go."

Mom takes Madison's hand and leads her out of the room. I walk toward my closet, completely forgetting not to go near the bed.

CHOMP! The shark lunges out from under it and clamps its jaws around my ankle.

"Come on, Lacey!" Mom yells.

I tug on the shark, but its mouth has opened so wide that its jaws meet on the other side of my ankle. I pull and I pry.

"Lacey! Right now! I mean it!"

———

I spend the rest of the night with a toy shark on my leg. We tell everyone at the restaurant that it's the "catch of the day," and Dad sells a lot of extra fish-and-chips because of it.

He wants me to wear the shark all the time.

When I get home, I find that Katarina has pulled my Endangered Animals calendar onto the floor. She stands right in the middle of it looking up at me.

"It's about time you got home! We need to discuss your training schedule!"

"Can I take my jacket off first?"

"No." Katarina points at a date on the calendar. "The play is eight days away and so is the full moon. Between now and then, we need to fix Paige's voice, get her the part of Cinderella, and make sure nothing goes wrong with the performance. Understand?"

I nod.

"We're just lucky *Cinderella* is on such an insane schedule. Eight days to stage a musical—madness!"

"It was supposed to be six weeks. But Mr. Griffith messed up."

"Mr. Griffith's not my problem, *you're* my problem. You're a hopeless amateur with the wand." Katarina pulls herself up to her full three-inch height. "But no one ever accused Katarina Sycorax of being a quitter. I'll train you from the second you get home from school tomorrow till you drop with exhaustion Sunday night. And if you listen to every single word I say, you might, just might, be able to use the wand by Monday."

I look at the calendar, suddenly feeling scared. It *is* just eight days till the play. But eight days is over a week. And you can do a lot in a week, right?

CHAPTER 11

Friday morning is sunny and bright, so when I show up to school in a raincoat, I get some funny looks. (I can't tell the other kids it's in case of a pigeon attack.) Luckily for me, everyone is distracted anyway, because Mr. Griffith is standing at the music room door taping up a piece of paper that says *Cinderella Cast List*. The second he steps away, the wannabe actors swarm in to look.

A girl starts shrieking so loud that I'm surprised it doesn't set off car alarms in the teachers' parking lot.

The shrieker, a girl named Ann Estey, jumps up and down like she'll never stop. "I'm Cinderella! I'm Cinderella! I'm Cinderella!"

Her friends hug her and jump up and down, too. "You're Cinderella! You're Cinderella! You're Cinderella!"

If this had happened last week, I would have thought, *Great!*

Ann Estey got the part! I don't know Ann all that well, but she seems pretty nice. She's always been a quiet girl—at least before she started shrieking—but her singing voice must be really great. Otherwise, Mr. Griffith wouldn't have chosen her ahead of all those tiara-wearing, one-shoed girls.

Did Paige get a part at all? I push my way through the crowd and look at the list. Just like Sunny and I thought, Scott Dearden is going to be Prince Charming. And sure enough, Chloe Martin is playing the fairy godmother. I skim past the names of the kids playing the ugly stepsisters and the other big parts. Way down at the bottom is Dancing Mouse Number Four. And that's the part Paige got.

I wonder what Paige is feeling right now. Maybe she hasn't seen the list, but I bet every single one of her friends has texted her about it. Messages that are all "Ooh, I'm so sorry," but are really just rubbing it in. That's got to be hard.

If it were me, I would be hiding in the janitor's bathroom on the second floor. I did that once when I farted during flute practice and totally ruined "Clair de Lune." I snuck out the back of the class and cried in the bathroom until the end of the day. (Later, Sunny said that no one even thought it was me. They thought it was Mrs. Holmes, the band teacher, who had been telling everyone about her new diet where she only eats broccoli.)

Paige *might* be in the janitor's bathroom. I know I'm not wand-trained yet, but I could try to talk to her and make her feel better. That's probably part of a fairy godmother's job, right?

I go up to the second-floor bathroom and find two stalls with closed doors, but no feet in either one. This is such a stupid idea. There's no way Paige Harrington would be in here. That would mean she's a little like me, and we all know she's not.

I turn to go, but then I hear a faint sniffle from one of the stalls. With my luck it's a rat with a cold who heard about me from the pigeons.

There's another sniffle. "Hello?" I call.

Two feet suddenly appear at the bottom of the stall. They're wearing really cute shoes.

"Paige, is that you? It's me, Lacey. Are you all right?"

The cute shoes don't move. And Paige says, "Yes, I'm all right. Now, leave me alone."

"But I think I know how you feel!"

"LEAVE ME ALONE!"

Wow! If Paige talked to Katarina like that, she'd get zapped with boils and oozing sores.

I give it another try. "Paige? Do you need some Kleenex?"

The stall door slams open and Paige stomps out of the bathroom and out of sight. It's going to be really hard to be her fairy godmother.

At the end of school, Sunny waits for me by my locker. "Okay, so today's the big day," she says.

My head is full of fairy godmothers, and Paige, and angry animals. Whatever Sunny's talking about has been erased from my mind, so I stall: "Yeah, the big day."

"And you don't think they're going to make my eyes look too small?"

I think I remember what she's talking about. "A lot of kids get glasses. Their eyes look fine."

Maybe I was wrong about the glasses, because Sunny seems hurt and mad all at the same time. She says, "You forgot. I can't believe you forgot."

"I did not!"

"You did, too. You completely forgot that today's the day we're going to the mall, and I'm getting bangs."

Bangs. Right. Sunny has been talking about them for six months. And I promised to go with her to the salon to make sure they don't butcher her. But I've got wand lessons as soon as I get home!

So I have to tell Sunny a big lie, and it's the first time I've told her a big lie since we've been best friends, and that's forever. Sure, I've told her little lies, the kind friends are supposed to tell. Like saying her new braces are almost invisible. Or that a C+ in English is practically a B. But I've never told a lie that matters. I say, "I'm really sorry, but my mom is sick, and I'm supposed to go right home and help with Madison."

Sunny doesn't suspect anything, she just looks worried. "I'll come keep you company! We can do the bangs tomorrow."

I know I've got wand lessons all weekend and won't have time for Sunny. So I do the math in my head and say, "My mom's got the seventy-two-hour flu! She doesn't want anyone but the family in the house. We're practically quarantined."

"Oh."

"You'd better go without me. And don't worry, the people at the salon are professionals. Bangs are their job."

"I don't know . . ."

"Trust me, you'll be fine!"

If Sunny had my problems, she wouldn't be worrying about hair.

"Color new! Pea turn blue!" Katarina chants.

"That's not much of a spell, is it?" I say. We're in the kitchen, staring at a single frozen pea that I took from the freezer. Katarina stands on my shoulder, and I can't help noticing that her wings don't seem to be healing very well. If anything, they look even more droopy and sad than yesterday.

Katarina says, "You have to learn the basics. Transformation spells are the key to being a good fairy godmother."

"So why don't I do something harder? Cinderella's godmother turned a pumpkin into a coach. Let me turn the pea into a moped, or even just a tricycle. Madison would like that."

"No. Turn the pea blue. That's enough."

"This is stupid."

"Do it!"

I raise the little wand and aim it at the pea: "Color new! Pea turn blue!" And the pea explodes with a little popping sound, *PLURP!* I have to wipe a speck of green pea goo off my face.

Katarina gives me an "I told you so" look. "That pea could have been Paige's head. That's why you have to learn the basics."

Paige is not my favorite person, but I don't want to make her explode. So, for the next hour, I say "Color new, pea turn blue" again and again and zap pea after pea.

PLURP! PLURP! PLURP! Every single one of them blows up until it looks like World War Pea in here. The counter, the floor, and I all get coated in pea innards.

Katarina somehow manages to stay spotless while she watches one of those daytime talk shows where people toss chairs at each other. After every *PLURP,* she just says, "Again!" in a bored little voice. She's not even looking at me.

And I try so many times that my wrist gets sore and every muscle in my body tenses up.

"For Pete's sake! Just toss it!" For a moment, I think Katarina's talking to the people on the TV. (Two women are *very* mad at their boyfriends.)

But no, she's looking at me. "*Toss it.* Think about what you want the wand to do, and then imagine using it to toss the spell where you want it to go."

Why didn't she tell me that fifty peas ago? Besides, if the

wand did what I was really thinking right now, Katarina would be in big trouble.

She says, "I thought you were one in a million. Obviously, I was wrong. You're not even one in one."

I'll admit it, that stings a little. I look at the pea, think blue thoughts, and toss the spell.

For the first time all afternoon, the pea doesn't explode, but turns a beautiful shade of sky blue. "Katarina! I did it!"

Katarina doesn't even look away from the TV. "Finally. Now, blue up another hundred peas."

"But I know how to do the spell!"

"Tell that to Paige when her head blows up."

This is a good point, so I count off peas as I zap them blue. By number sixty-seven, I'm so bored I can barely keep my eyes open. By number ninety-two, I think I actually do fall asleep for a second, just as I'm tossing the spell. My hand wiggles a tiny bit, so I miss the pea and accidentally aim at the shiny metal toaster on the counter next to it. An instant later, my face turns warm and tingly. I pat it. It feels normal enough.

Then I get a glimpse of myself in the toaster: just like the peas, my face is a beautiful shade of sky blue. I shout "KATARINA!" and she looks over at me, not a bit surprised. "Did I not mention that you have to be extra careful around shiny objects?"

"No!"

"I thought I did. You need to be extra careful around shiny objects. Spells can bounce!"

"Now you tell me! I'm BLUE!" I rub my face, hoping the color will rub off. If anything, it just gets bluer.

Then, like things aren't bad enough, a car door slams in the driveway. I look out and see Mom and Madison getting out of the car. I'm blue, and the kitchen still looks like World War Pea.

I grab paper towels and wipe pea slime off the counter, the refrigerator, the floor, and the ceiling fan. I've never worked this fast in my life. As I stuff the last paper towel in the garbage can, I think, *I did it!* Except, I forgot one thing.

Mom comes through the door. "Lacey! Why are you blue?"

And Madison says, "Pretty! I want to be blue, too!"

Mom waits for my answer, more curious than worried. (She's a very calm mom.)

Katarina peers out from behind the TV, covering her mouth with her hand and trying not to laugh.

Thinking hard, I finally tell Mom, "I'm trying out for the school play. There's a part for a bluebird."

To my surprise, Mom buys this. "Great, honey. That sounds fun." But when she squints at me, I'm worried that she's figured out it's not makeup, it's magic. Then she breaks into a big grin. "And at the restaurant tonight you can push the blueberry pie! Maybe we'll even put you out front with a sign!"

Katarina GUFFAWS. I have to cough to cover up the sound.

At a couple of minutes to midnight, Katarina and I sit in my bedroom staring at the clock and waiting for the blue spell to wear off. While the seconds tick by, I ask Katarina a question that's been bothering me: "Why doesn't everyone have a fairy godmother?"

"Why doesn't everyone win the lottery?"

"I'm serious."

"And so am I. There are millions of needy girls out there, and only a few fairy godmothers. We do the very best we can, but you have a better chance of being simultaneously hit by lightning and run over by a bus than of getting a fairy godmother."

"So, Paige was the big winner. Typical."

"Yep, until you ruined it for her."

I look at my blue face in the mirror. "Are you positive it's going to wear off?"

She's crawled into the jewelry box, pulling her battered wings around her like blankets. "Maybe not. Why do you think Pinocchio's Blue Fairy is blue?"

I'm horrified. "Because she bounced a spell off a toaster?"

Katarina rolls her eyes. I wish she'd stop doing that. "I'm joking! For one thing, they didn't have toasters in nineteenth-century Italy. For another, I know the Blue Fairy. She's not blue like the color, she's blue like she's clinically depressed. A *very* sad girl."

Katarina suddenly goes goggle-eyed with shock: "Jiminy Cricket! Look at your face!"

I whip around to the mirror. The sky blue has gone from my face, and it's pink again. I look back at Katarina and see her smirking. "Dimwit," she says. And then she shuts the jewelry box lid.

CHAPTER 13

Saturday morning, my eyes pop open, and I look at the clock. It's 5:00 a.m.—why am I awake? I close my eyes again, and then Katarina pulls up my left eyelid and peers in. When you're still almost asleep, it's very disturbing to have a cranky little woman looking into your eyeball from half an inch away.

"Wake up! We've got work to do!" she says. "And get me some coffee!"

I moan and roll over. "I'm too sleepy."

"*Get me some coffee!*" she repeats. When I keep ignoring her, she sticks her head in my ear and starts humming the 1812 Overture as loud as she can. That's the one that goes *DA-DA-DA-DA-DA-DA-DA-DA-DA! DA-DA-DA-DA-DA-DA-DA-DA-DA!* and then has a couple of cymbal crashes. But instead of cymbal crashes, Katarina snorts really loud.

You try sleeping through the 1812 Overture when it's being performed in your ear by a cranky fairy who wants coffee.

Saturday morning, 6:00 a.m.:

"Go get some rags so we can practice making dresses," Katarina says, sipping from the toothpaste cap full of coffee I got her.

"We don't have any rags. How about paper towels?"

"Fairy godmothers can make dresses out of anything."

I get a roll of towels and Katarina gives me the spell: "Out of litter make a dress that glitters!"

"Does it have to? Glitter got us into this mess," I say.

"Yes!"

"Why?"

"A good dress glitters. Read your fairy tales."

I think my first try at paper-towel-into-dress actually looks okay. Sure, it doesn't glitter much. Well, not at all. But it has armholes and a neck hole and everything. Katarina's only comment is to blow her nose in it very loudly. She is so rude!

The bed gets stacked with rejected dresses: the sleeves are too long, the hems are too short, the sashes don't sash. And, worst of all, the glitter doesn't glitter.

I tell Katarina we should just conjure up a credit card and go to the mall, but she points at the paper towels and tells me to keep practicing. So I try it fifty-two more times; the room gets so crammed with ugly paper-towel dresses we can hardly move.

Finally, Katarina throws a tantrum. "You're setting fashion back five hundred years! I made better dresses in the Dark Ages! And in the Dark Ages we didn't have paper towels! We didn't even have rags! We used *dirt*! And the dresses made from dirt were *lovely*!" She's so mad she starts jumping up and down on the bed, which is not a good thing to do when you're three inches tall and there's a tower of paper towel dresses rising above you.

"Watch out!" I say.

Too late. The dresses fall on top of her, and she disappears from view.

Gone, but not silent. She shrieks, "You're hopeless! Do you hear me? HOPELESS!"

Saturday afternoon, 12:15 p.m.:
But I'm not so hopeless that we don't go on to the next lesson, which involves hours in the basement trying to turn vegetables into vehicles.

I try. I really do. But the closest I get is turning a green pepper into a skateboard with little legs instead of wheels.

The skateboard scampers all over the basement like a clumsy puppy, and I laugh out loud when it tosses Katarina into the air as if she's the best dog toy ever.

"Go away!" she says. "Bad skateboard! Bad!"

Instead, the skateboard scoops her up onto its back and scampers in circles while Katarina hangs on by her fingernails. "Put me down!"

I finally catch the skateboard and pull Katarina off. When Julius was being a bad kitten, I used to cuddle him and sing him to sleep. The skateboard is almost a puppy, so I cuddle it and sing, *"Go to sleep, go to sleep, go to sleep, little skateboard. . . ."*

Katarina shakes her head. "Oh, *please!*"

Ten minutes and a hundred choruses of "go to sleep" later, the skateboard snoozes in my lap, its little legs curled up contentedly.

I see that Katarina's gone to sleep, too, so I gently shake her. She wakes up with a start: "I wasn't sleeping," she says. "I was resting my eyes! On to the next lesson!"

Saturday afternoon, 4:30 p.m.:
When we're back in my room, squeezed in between stacks of paper-towel dresses, Katarina tells me to find a rat to turn into a footman.

"What's a footman?" I ask.

"I'm constantly amazed at the ignorance of this modern age. It's like IQ points drop every century."

I can't help being snarky. "Maybe I'll know what a footman is when *I* get to be five hundred years old."

Katarina lights up with pleasure and stares at herself in the mirror: "You really think I only look five hundred?" To be honest, she looks exhausted; even her wings seem tired. But I'm not going to tell her that.

Then she says, in a much happier tone, "A footman is a personal servant. He opens doors, carries luggage, stands behind you at dinner, and polishes the silver. They're very handy. Now, find a rat!"

"We don't have any rats." I glance down at the windowsill. "How about an ant?"

Katarina sighs. "It's better than nothing. Say, 'On count of three, a footman you will be.'"

So I try it over and over and over again for what seems like forever. The ant is really small; besides, hitting a moving target is hard.

Finally, the spell hits the ant perfectly on his little head. There's a flash of light, and a tiny man no bigger than Katarina appears. He's dressed in a blue satin suit and wears a white wig.

"Look, Katarina! I did it! I did it!"

When there's no answer, I turn to find Katarina sound asleep on my pillow, snoring even louder than usual.

And just then Mom calls from the kitchen, "Lacey! Dinner's on the table!"

As soon as the little footman hears "dinner," he springs to attention and says, in a tiny, helium-high voice, "Milady! I shall serve you!" I grab him as he runs for the door.

"You have to stay here," I say.

"Must serve you! Must serve you! Must serve you!" He scrambles out of my hand, reaches the door, and tries to squeeze under it. Geez. Mom doesn't notice everything, but she's sure to see a three-inch-tall footman in satin. (Plus, Julius will probably eat him.) I have to think fast. "Footman! Stop!"

"Must serve you! Must serve you!"

"You can serve me by . . . polishing the silver! It's an urgent life-or-death silver-polishing crisis!"

He turns, intrigued. "Must polish silver! Must polish silver! Must polish silver."

If you only had an ant-sized brain, you wouldn't be very smart, either.

I pick him up and put him back down on the dresser, where Katarina tossed all my jewelry. His eyes open wide at the sight of my fake silver chains and bracelets. "Oooh," he says, like he just walked into the vault at Tiffany's. He sits right down, pulls a tiny rag out of his pocket, and starts to polish. This is going to take him all night. *Good.*

I try to shake Katarina awake, but she snores some more and rolls over. I'm worried about her. What if she's catching a cold? Think how cranky she'll be *then*!

Hoping all she needs is a good night's sleep, I gently put her into the jewelry box and close the lid. "Good night, Katarina."

Next to the jewelry box, the footman keeps polishing.

Saturday evening, 8:00 p.m.:

I babysit Madison while Mom and Dad are at the restaurant. She wanted to watch the Sleeping Beauty cartoon for the one-billionth time. I figured I could learn something useful, so I let her.

Usually, Julius sits on my lap whenever we watch a movie, kneading my shirt with his paws and purring. But tonight he just glares at me from the doorway. I know that animals hate me, but Julius isn't just an animal—he's family. And seeing him like this makes me so sad I want to cry.

I try to stop thinking about it and concentrate on the movie. On the TV, the part where the fairies turn the gown from pink to blue and back again comes on, and Madison laughs like she always does.

"That's a lot harder than it looks," I say.

Saturday evening, 11:59 p.m.:

I sit in my bedroom so tired I can barely keep my eyes open, but I really want to see the dresses change back at midnight—not to mention the footman. He's still polishing the "silver," and my jewelry has never looked better. But even if I did want to fall asleep, there's no room on the dress-covered bed.

Katarina snores in the jewelry box as I watch the seconds tick away on my clock. 11:59:57. 11:59:58. 11:59:59.

12:00.

A faint breath of wind blows past me, and the sixty-seven dresses in the room are replaced by sixty-seven paper towels that flutter down to the floor like leaves. It's too bad Julius refuses to come into my room. He would have really liked chasing them.

The newly restored ant climbs along a silver necklace, looking confused. I pick the necklace up and move him to the windowsill. If ants dream, he's going to think he's been having a weird one.

As I crawl into bed, I look at the clock and realize we've got exactly a week to go. A week minus three minutes, to be exact. I better get some sleep. As hard as today was, I know Katarina's going to have ten times more for me to do tomorrow.

CHAPTER
14

I'm still asleep when Mom comes into my room the next morning. "Wake up, lazybones. It's late!"

I'm surprised to see sun pouring into the room. It's 10:30! I was expecting Katarina to start pulling my eyelids open at the crack of dawn, but she must have overslept, too. We've wasted hours! What about our schedule?

Mom looks at the paper towels on the floor. "*This* is where my paper towels went! What have you been doing in here?"

"Top secret project for the school play. I'm on the stage crew."

"You are?"

"Yes, didn't I tell you?"

Mom buys my lie—*another* one! I know it's all for a good cause, but I still feel guilty about lying. She says, "Well, if you end up not using them, stack them up and bring them back to the kitchen."

As soon as Mom leaves, I hurry over to the dresser and tap on the closed lid of the jewelry box. "Hello? Katarina? Are you awake?"

There's no answer from inside. I tap again. "Katarina? It's ten thirty! Get up!"

Still no answer. I pull open the jewelry-box lid, expecting to find a cranky little fairy who needs her coffee.

Instead, I find a cocoon. It's about the size of Katarina, maybe a little bigger, and it's absolutely beautiful. The metallic-looking surface shimmers in the light with hazy ripples of blue and green and the faintest pink. Like it's going to become the world's most beautiful butterfly.

But I don't need the world's most beautiful butterfly—I need Katarina! We've got work to do!

Tapping very gently on the surface of the cocoon, I say, "Katarina?" When there's no answer, I put my ear close to it and hear something that's very faint and far away. At first, I think it's the sound of the ocean, like when you put a seashell up to your ear. A very soft *Roarr! Roarrr! Rooaaarr!*

But it's not the ocean. It's Katarina snoring inside.

I try to figure out what's going on. The night we met, she said something about cocooning, but why now? Katarina did seem super tired and droopy yesterday. Maybe cocooning is a fairy's way of healing herself.

But how long is it going to take?

I start Googling. Wikipedia says a cocoon stage can last *days, weeks, or even years*. Thanks for being specific, Wikipedia!

That was sarcasm.

Wikipedia also says that most butterflies come out of their cocoons right at sunrise. Maybe I'll be lucky, and Katarina will be good as new first thing tomorrow morning. We'll be a day behind schedule, but I think that still leaves us enough time to get Paige her dream and get us out of trouble.

I sure hope so.

So, instead of having to spend Sunday doing more wand training, I've got the day free. I think about calling Sunny and hanging out with her, but that would mean even more lying. It's better to let her go on thinking Mom's got the flu. I'll make it up to her at school tomorrow.

I end up sitting on the couch all day watching football with Dad. He's always desperate for a football buddy in this house full of girls. I've spent so many years pretending to be interested that I know a lot about the game—which teams are which, who the players are, and how it's all about blocking. But today I'm distracted, worrying about Katarina. So I jump a little when Dad shouts, "What a play! Look at that guy dance!"

Mom sticks her head in the doorway looking hopeful.

"Dancing?" She's disappointed when she sees it's just football.

Then Madison comes running in. "We're dancing?" She raises her arms and spins and spins and spins in front of the TV like a crazy ballerina. "I could do this *forever*!"

Mom giggles, and Dad sighs as he misses a touchdown.

Poor Dad.

CHAPTER

15

Please, I say to myself.

Then I add in five more pleases just to be safe.

It's first thing Monday morning, and I'm hoping that Katarina is back in the land of the uncocooned. I slowly open the jewelry box.

Nooooo! The cocoon looks exactly the same as it did when I checked it last night: not a smudge, not a crack.

What am I going to do? I need help! If only I could tell Sunny about what's going on. Sure, she's no good in a crisis, but this is beyond crisis! This is . . .

. . . *bad.*

I need my best friend. The second I see Sunny, I'm going to tell her the whole story.

I find Sunny in the hallway at school. She's got her head in her locker, hunting for something.

"Sunny! I need to talk you!"

She just leans even deeper into her locker. "But I don't want to talk to you. Ever."

She sounds mad—*really* mad. Madder than I've ever heard her. I say, "What's wrong?"

Sunny doesn't say a single word. She just straightens up and looks at me.

I can't help it. I gasp out loud.

She points at her bangs: "And this is after my mom tried to fix them!" Her bangs are short, uneven, and point in funny directions, like exclamation points that got loose and landed on her

head. Sunny was worried about the salon butchering her hair, but even butchering would have been better than this.

After seeing Sunny's bangs, my problems don't seem nearly as bad.

Sunny takes the stocking cap she was searching for out of her locker and says, "This is all your fault."

"But, Sunny—"

"I'm not talking to you till my hair grows back."

"I'm so sorry!"

Sunny pulls the cap down over her head and stomps away.

I'm a horrible friend.

In math class, Mrs. Patel stands up front talking about our assignment, but I don't hear a word she's saying, because my mind is so full of my problems. My best friend has stopped speaking to me, and I'm a fairy-godmother-in-training without a trainer. . . .

What if Katarina doesn't wake up in time? Even if she does, we missed a whole day of wand training yesterday. And we've only got till Saturday!

Mom always feels better about things when she makes a list, so I open my notebook. After I make sure that nobody is looking over my shoulder, I write, *Fairy Godmother To Do*, and start listing:

1) Fix Paige's singing voice.
2) Get rid of Ann Estey.

3) Get Paige the part.

4) Make sure nothing goes wrong with the play on Saturday night.

I think I'm done, and then I remember one more thing. I add:

5) Fix things with Sunny.

Hmm . . . I don't know what Mom's talking about. Writing out this list doesn't make me feel better at all. In fact, I feel worse.

Let's start with number 1. I may be able to turn Paige's singing voice blue, but I don't know how to make it sound good. And number 2, getting rid of Ann Estey: even if I can do it, is that fair? Ann's a nice girl who finally got her big chance. Now I'm supposed to take it away from her just to give Paige the part? (It was easier in the Cinderella story, because you hated the stepsisters so much. This shows why real life is so much more complicated than fairy tales.) And number 3 depends on number 1. Number 4 depends on number 3. Number 5—which is the most important one of all—probably won't get solved till Sunny's hair grows out. How am I supposed to make everything work?

"*Lacey!*"

I jump in my seat and look up to see Mrs. Patel staring at me with her eyebrows raised. All the kids are looking at me, too. This must mean she just asked me a question about the equation she's written on the board.

I give the only answer I can: "Mrs. Patel, I just can't do it." And unless Katarina wakes up, that's the truth.

CHAPTER 16

I know there's a rehearsal for the play after school, so I stop by the auditorium to check things out. With less than a week to go, there's a big crazy rush in here today. Kids paint scenery, build walls, aim lights, sew costumes, and yell at each other. Yell a *lot*. It makes the Hungry Moose seem like the library.

I see that Ann Estey has just walked onto the stage, so I slip into a seat to watch. I'm hoping that she'll be bad. If she's bad, it won't be such a rotten thing to replace her with Paige. Maybe she'll sing too loud. Maybe she'll sing too soft. Maybe she'll forget the words.

She doesn't do any of these. She sings like an angel.

There's a hush in the auditorium as people stop yelling and hammering and sewing to listen to her. It's the prettiest singing I've ever heard.

Perfect note after perfect note comes out of Ann's throat,

and I know she must love to sing more than anything else in the world. I would be the worst person ever if I took this part away from her.

After Ann finishes the song, everyone applauds and whistles, and she blushes. She's not only talented, she's humble! Mr. Griffith looks up from the piano, his eyes open for once. He says, "Thank you, Ann. I didn't think it was possible, but you made my song sound even better." No one ever accused Mr. Griffith of being humble.

He looks offstage. "All right! Dancing mice, front and center! Where are my dancing mice!"

Paige and three other girls walk to the middle of the stage. They don't have their costumes yet, but they wear felt mouse ears and have tails made out of rope. Paige looks absolutely miserable. There's no trace of an invisible spotlight on her today. How could it shine through those ugly ears?

"All right, let's work on the mouse dance! Remember, you're simple peasant mice, so nothing fancy." The girls start dancing around the stage. The other three girls look like they can barely walk, much less dance, but Paige has real grace. For a moment, that invisible spotlight turns back on.

"No, no, NO!" Mr. Griffith shouts. The girls freeze and look at him. "Paige, what are you doing! I said *simple*! Blend in with the other girls!"

He looks a little closer at her face. "And what are you doing with your makeup? That red eyeliner is all wrong. We're doing musical theater, not Greek tragedy."

I stare at Paige. Her eyes aren't red from eyeliner, they're red from crying. I wouldn't be surprised if someone told me she's been crying all weekend.

At home that night, I sit in my bedroom staring at Katarina's cocoon, thinking.

If only I hadn't caught Katarina in my hair . . .

If only Julius hadn't eaten Katarina and hurt her shoulder and mangled her wings . . . I wouldn't be facing worldwide animal hatred right now.

Plus, Sunny would still be my best friend.

And Paige would have her fairy godmother, and she would be on her way to getting her dream. But all she has right now is me.

If Katarina would just break out of the cocoon and help me, I wouldn't care how cranky she is. I would do every single thing she tells me and be happy about it.

I put my ear next to the cocoon, listening like I did before. And I hear a voice saying, "Lacey, you're going to have to take that wand and do it all yourself. It's up to you."

And I realize that the voice isn't coming from inside the cocoon, it's coming from inside me.

I don't want to listen, but I have to.

CHAPTER 17

As I leave for school in the morning, I have a thought: it's chilly in my room. What if that's why Katarina hasn't broken out yet? So I put the cocoon in my sweater pocket where it's warm. She can come with me.

I wait for Paige on the school's front steps (and pray there won't be any birds). After what seems like forever, Paige walks up with her cheerleader friends Makayla and Taylor. Have you noticed that popular girls always travel in packs? They're the wolves of middle school, and the rest of us are just rabbits trying not to get eaten.

Normally, I would never dream of interrupting Paige when she's with her pack; it's just not something a smart rabbit would do. But today I don't have time to be smart. As the three girls walk by I whisper, "Paige? Can I talk to you?"

Paige says, "What do you want, Underwear Girl?" And Makayla and Taylor giggle.

I bet Katarina never has to put up with stuff like this. I plead, "I need to talk to you about something personal."

Paige looks at me, on the verge of walking away, so I say, "It's really important. Please, Paige."

Paige tells Makayla and Taylor, "I'll meet you inside." Not a suggestion, an order. The girls smirk at me as they go in.

"What do you want?" Paige asks.

"I can't talk about it here. Can we go someplace?"

"No. Tell me what you want, or I'm leaving."

I'm so nervous that words just spew out of my mouth: "Remember that night I came to your house with takeout? Well, there was a moth next to your porch light. Only it wasn't a moth. It was your fairy godmother! But she got caught in my gluey hair. Remember, from the poster? You really should use less glitter glue. It's very dangerous. Anyhow, I got her home and cleaned her up, and Julius ate her. But don't worry, he spit her out again. But then her wand arm didn't work. And her wings needed to heal, too. So she cocooned! And . . . ta-da! Now I'm your fairy godmother."

Paige looks at me, completely speechless.

"I've got things entirely under control. I know you want the lead in the play. So, let's make that happen!"

Paige steps back as if she's in danger of catching mental cooties from me.

"I can prove it. Look! I have a wand!" I reach into my pocket and pull out the wand. It looks like I'm holding a toothpick, but it's the best I can do.

This is the moment where Paige should say, "Awesome! What's next?" But she just looks confused. What can I do to convince her?

I know! I dig deeper into my pocket and pull out Katarina's cocoon. "Look! Here she is! If you put it up to your ear you can hear her snoring!" I hold it out to Paige . . .

. . . who pulls away like I'm trying to hand her dog poop. She says, "One more word from you, and I'm telling Principal Nazarino!"

I think about saying, *Wait! Wait! You've got to listen to me!* But then I realize those are words, so I keep quiet.

Paige scurries up the steps and disappears inside.

That could have gone better.

When I sit down next to Sunny in homeroom, she's still wearing a hat and an angry expression. Usually Sunny would have forgiven me by now, but I guess you shouldn't mess with a girl's hair.

Gaby Thompson, who is the school's biggest gossip, leans toward me and whispers, "Is it true?"

"Is what true?"

"That you pulled a knife on Paige Harrington outside school."

"It wasn't a knife! It was—" I stop myself; it's not like I can tell people it was a wand.

Rick Malcolm chimes in, "Blaine Anders told me that you're going to get kicked out of school!"

This is too much for Sunny, butchered bangs and all. She says, "Blaine Anders also said that the water in the drinking fountain comes straight from the toilet. He lies about everything."

Rick says, "But he's not lying about Lacey getting kicked out of school."

No one would be stupid enough to believe that I had a knife, right?

Then Principal Nazarino strides into the room. She hasn't come into homeroom since . . . since never.

I think, *Please don't let this be about me.*

Principal Nazarino stands in front of the class. "Lacey Unger-Ware! Come here, please."

My heart starts pounding three hundred beats a minute. Walking up to the principal on shaky legs, I expect her to whip out handcuffs. So when Principal Nazarino puts her arm around me, I can't help flinching.

To my surprise, she grins and tells the class, "We here at Lincoln Middle School should all be very proud of Lacey! I've just found out she's one of the five finalists for the Highland Park Zoo intern contest."

I give her a surprised Scooby-Doo look. I might as well have said, *Hrwha?*

Principal Nazarino says, "Lincoln hasn't had a finalist in over ten years. Now we're finally going to kick Harry S. Truman Middle School's butt!"

Wow. She's taking this zoo intern thing very personally.

She says, "The interview is tomorrow. So Lacey, get a lot of sleep tonight and make us even prouder! You're a role model for us all!"

Sunny applauds, and for a long, long moment, she's the only one. But then Gaby Thompson joins in. A second or two later, the whole room is applauding and stomping.

I know this is less about me than it is about the fun of making a lot of noise during school hours—and in front of the principal. But still, I've gone from juvenile delinquent to role model in less than sixty seconds. That's got to be some kind of record. For a little while, I just listen to the applause and enjoy it.

Then a picture creeps into my brain, only it's more like a movie. I see me at the zoo, very snazzily dressed in a zoo intern vest. I'm leading a group of kindergartners through the bear habitat. The little kids all stare at me adoringly as I stop in front of the polar bear cage and start telling them everything I know about bears, which is a lot. A moment later, *CRASH! ROAR!* The polar bear bursts through the bars and bites my head off.

You can imagine what that looks like. I would describe it to you, but you'd totally barf. Trust me. It's *gross*.

This very educational movie is reminding me that I can't be a zoo intern if every animal in the world hates me. I can't even go to the zoo. I look up at Principal Nazarino and say, "I can't do the interview tomorrow."

The applause stops. Principal Nazarino frowns at me. "Of course you can."

"Next week would be much better for me."

"Don't be ridiculous. You *must* do the interview tomorrow. Don't you want to kick Harry S. Truman Middle School's butt?"

Sure I do. But I also don't want the polar bear to bite my head off.

I've got to fix Paige's voice *soon*. Maybe if I can get Paige partway to her dream, the animals will only hate me . . .

. . . partway.

CHAPTER
18

In English class, while all the other kids read *To Kill a Mockingbird*, I work on a spell to change Paige's voice. I want her to sing better than Ann Estey. But nothing rhymes with Estey. "Testy," maybe. But that's not helping me any.

Ann sings like an angel, and that's what I want for Paige. A beautiful, angelic singing voice. But what rhymes with *angel*?

I write in my notebook: *Angelic you sing, with plenty of zing.* Ugh.

I try, *Best voice in school, makes every kid drool.*

It *could* work—and then I imagine hundreds of kids magically drooling. That's disgusting.

I keep thinking. Finally, I write, *For a change you'll sing like an angel.*

Hmm . . . that's not terrible; in fact, that's pretty good.

Magic time!

For the rest of the day, I try to sneak up on Paige and toss the spell at her. I pass her in the hall right before lunch, but there are too many other kids in the way.

Then, between fifth and sixth periods, I see her leaning down over the drinking fountain. Feeling like a lion stalking a gazelle at a watering hole, I slowly creep toward Paige.

When I'm two steps away, I raise my wand. "For a change you'll—"

Ooofff! Somebody bumps into me, and I drop the wand. Paige gets away. *Darn it!*

As I squat on the floor of the busy hallway and feel around for the wand, someone crouches down by me and says, "What are we looking for?"

I turn, and Scott Dearden's beautiful eyes are a foot away from mine. I stop breathing. Oh my God—he's talking to me! That means I need to say something back. What should I say? *What should I say?* "You have the longest eyelashes!" comes out of my mouth.

Oh.

No.

Let me die now.

But he just smiles. "Yeah. I'm a freak."

"You're not a freak!" I steady myself with my hand, and

something sharp pokes into my thumb. "OW!" It's the wand.

"You all right?" Scott asks.

"Found it! My earring, I mean!"

We both stand up again. Scott says, "See you around," and vanishes into the crowd. Scott Dearden just talked to me, and he must think I'm an idiot.

I catch up to Paige at play rehearsal after school and watch from behind a painted fireplace as she practices her mouse dance with the other girls. With Mr. Griffith's coaching, she's now just as bad as the rest of them. *Clomp! Clomp! Clomp! Squeak! Squeak! Squeak!* Somebody needs to call an exterminator and put them out of their misery.

Mr. Griffith nods approvingly. "Very good, girls! The dance is getting just that quality of postmodern ennui I'm looking for."

If *ennui* means "really sucky," he's absolutely right.

My chance finally comes when the girls clomp offstage. I've got a clear shot at Paige! I raise the wand and quietly chant, "For a change you'll sing like an angel."

Just as Katarina taught me, I toss the spell right at her.

Nothing happens. *Nothing.* As a fairy godmother, I'm full of ennui.

Mr. Griffith calls, "Paige, I've been thinking. Can you add one more squeak after the third turn?"

Paige opens her mouth; instead of answering his question, she sings, *"GLO! OH-OH-OH! OH-OH-OH! RIA!"*

OMG! It worked! My spell worked! It's the most beautiful singing I've ever heard! She sounds like an angel!

Paige clutches her throat, totally confused about what's happening.

Mr. Griffith leaps onto the stage and rushes up to her. "Do that again."

She hesitates.

"I said, do it again!"

She opens her mouth, and the same angelic sounds come out. *"GLO! OH-OH-OH! OH-OH-OH! RIA!"*

I am *so* good!

As Mr. Griffith paces around Paige, you can almost see the wheels turning in his head. Is he tempted to give Paige the part instead of Ann? He says, "Paige, sing 'I've Lost My Shoe and You.'" He's tempted, all right.

Paige sings, *"GLO! OH-OH-OH! OH-OH-OH! RIA!"*

"Enough of that. Sing 'I've Lost My Shoe.'"

Paige's mouth opens and forms an *I* shape. She struggles a little, and then the same thing as before comes out: *"GLO! OH-OH-OH! OH-OH-OH! RIA!"*

Uh-oh. On the plus side, my spell worked. On the minus side, angels seem to sing only one thing.

Mr. Griffith's face turns red. "Sing 'I've Lost My Shoe.'"

Paige, looking panicky, uses her hands to force her mouth into the *I* shape. There's a long, long pause, and then she sings, *"GLO! OH-OH-OH! OH-OH-OH! RIA!"*

Mr. Griffith's face is *really* red now. "Is this a joke? Paige, what are you doing?"

She points at her throat and shakes her head.

"Are you mocking me?"

Paige makes one last, desperate attempt to sing something,

say something different. But all that comes out is *"GLO! OH-OH-OH! OH-OH-OH! RIA!"* She bursts into tears and runs out of the auditorium. Who does she remind me of?

Oh, right. Cinderella running out of the ball. All she needs is a missing shoe.

CHAPTER

19

I rush through the halls searching for Paige. I even check the second-floor janitor's bathroom. Empty.

There's a big window at the top of the stairs, and I look through it out at the school grounds. At first, all I see is Makayla and Taylor practicing cheers at the edge of the football field. Then I see Paige running up to them waving her arms like a crazy person. I need to get down to the field fast.

The second I'm outside, I hear Paige's angelic voice floating toward me: *"GLO! OH-OH-OH! OH-OH-OH! RIA!"*

I run to the edge of the field, where Paige is pointing toward her throat. Her friends are totally confused by what's going on.

Makayla says, "Maybe she's playing charades."

Taylor asks, "Paige? Are you playing charades?"

Paige shakes her head no. She's starting to panic.

Makayla turns to Taylor. "Maybe she's got a brain tumor. I saw this HBO movie where this girl stopped talking and started barking. By the end, her boyfriend had to howl like a dog to tell her he loved her. And then she died."

Taylor looks horrified, but I can tell she also loves this idea. She says, "Paige? Bark twice if you have a brain tumor."

Paige sings, *"GLO! OH-OH-OH! OH-OH-OH! RIA!"*

The girls look even more confused. Finally, Makayla pulls out her cell phone. "There's only one thing we can do—put this on YouTube!"

That's so evil! It would be like me putting a picture of Sunny's bangs online. I can't let Makayla do this—a fairy god-mother would never allow YouTube humiliation.

So I walk up to Paige and grab her sleeve. "Paige? Your father is waiting for you out front."

Paige looks at me with relief.

Makayla's cell phone is raised and ready. "Come on, Paige! Sing your crazy song!" Instead, Paige runs off the field.

I catch up with Paige at the curb where parents wait in their cars to pick up their kids. She's looking up and down the street, hoping to see her father.

I say, "He's not here. I made that up to get you away from your friends."

She stares at me, her eyes full of questions. I tell her, "I'm so sorry about the singing thing. Being a fairy godmother is really hard."

This is *not* the answer Paige wants to hear.

"But at least I didn't blow your head up like a pea, or make you drool or something!" I tell her. "Angel singing's not so bad. And at midnight, you'll be normal again."

Paige pulls out her cell phone, types in a message, and holds it up for me to see. It says, *U R crazy. Get away from me!*

"I'm not crazy. It's magic! You have to believe me. And we don't have a lot of time. We really only have from now till Saturday!"

Paige just stomps away.

This would be a lot easier if I were three inches tall, with butterfly wings. When a person like that talks about magic, you go, *Wow!* But when I, Lacey Unger-Ware, talk about magic, you go, *U R crazy!*

You'd think that singing like an angel would convince anybody. But not Paige.

"Paige, stop! I'll prove it!"

She doesn't stop. It looks like she's going to stomp all the way home.

Then I see a garbage can, and I know what to do. Not with the garbage can, with the apple core that's sitting on top of it. I grab the core by the stem and say, "Watch this!"

If I'm very, very lucky, I can turn it into some kind of vehicle. I just hope it's not a skateboard with legs. I raise the wand and chant, "Door to door by apple core!"

I toss the spell, and the surface of the apple core glows like a hundred tubes of glitter. Paige's eyes open wide—Katarina's not the only one who can't resist things that sparkle.

The apple rises into the air and hovers for a moment or two. This is *sooo* cool! Then it smashes into the sidewalk, exploding in a shower of sparks.

When the sparks finally clear, we see a shiny new moped, complete with apple-red paint. I've done it! Fruit into vehicle, no problem.

Feeling pretty proud of myself, I tell her, "Hop on! I'll take you home."

Paige stares at the moped like she's dreaming. She closes her eyes and then opens them slowly, as if she expects it not to be there. I just give her a friendly wave. "Get on!" I pat the seat. "There's plenty of room."

The motor suddenly ROARS to life, way louder than I expected. It sounds like a jet engine.

Paige runs away with her hands clutching her ears.

ROAR! ROAR! The engine keeps revving. I try to jump off, but my rear end feels glued to the seat.

And then the moped starts to move. I must have hit the gas by mistake! I take my hands off the handlebars, which is not a good idea. It lurches forward, and I'm jerked back so far I'm almost lying flat on the seat.

The front wheel turns all by itself, and the moped charges at Paige like an angry bull. Even though I'm pumping the brakes, it doesn't slow down. "Watch out!" I shout.

When the moped barrels toward Paige, I'm sure she's going to be roadkill, so I close my eyes. There's a loud *THUMP*, and I let out a shriek. This is awful!

I peek out of one eye and see Paige riding on the handlebars. She got scooped up the way Katarina got scooped up by the skateboard.

ROARRR! The moped goes even faster, zooming us straight toward the brick wall of the fire station across the street. I scream, and Paige sings, *"GLO! OH-OH-OH! OH-OH-OH! RIA!"* It's the only sound she can make.

The brick wall is inches away. But we don't crash, we drive straight up the side of the wall. Let me say that again: we drive up the side of the wall! Straight up! Like it's nothing! Who made this thing? Spider-Man?

No, *I* did. I can't wait till Katarina wakes up so I can tell her about it.

Then we reach the roof, and we're back to boring old horizontal. Well, it *would* be boring if we weren't heading straight for the other side of the building.

I SCREAM. Paige is too scared now even to sing.

As we fly off into nothing, I feel like I left my stomach back on the roof.

And then we come down in a surprisingly soft landing. If this were an airplane, all the passengers would be applauding right now. We rush on, passing cars on the street in an apple-red blur.

The moped barrels toward the Shop 'n Save market and its big plate-glass windows. I brace myself, expecting to go straight up the wall again. What if the glass breaks and cuts us into hamburger?

At the last moment, the moped zigzags, and we shoot through the automatic doors and into the store.

WHUMP! We crash through a pyramid of potato chips.

THUMP! We send two hundred loaves of bread flying.

KERCHUNK! We knock the birthday cards from aisle six into aisle thirteen.

WHOOSH! We blow through the swinging doors in back, soar off the loading dock, and blast down another street, going what seems like a million miles an hour. Have you seen those pictures of astronauts going so fast that their cheeks are all pulled back? Well, that's us right now. I want to scream again, but the wind pushes the sound right back down my throat.

We head straight for a house, and I brace myself. What's it

going to be? Up the wall? Through the door? Down the chimney?

SCREEEEEEEEEEEEEECH!!!!! The moped stops right in front of the house and the jet sound fades away into a friendly little *putt-putt-putt*. We're parked on the front porch as if this were exactly where we were supposed to be.

This place looks familiar . . .

. . . because it's Paige's house. Door to door by apple core. There's a friendly "beep-beep" from the moped, and I can't help patting it. "Uh, thank you!" I tell it. The putt-putting sound becomes a happy purr.

"That wasn't so bad," I say. Then Paige turns around, and her face is completely covered with splattered bugs, some of them still wiggling. *Ewwwwwww.* She's been my windshield for the whole ride.

Paige is surprisingly calm. (I guess you don't get to be queen of the school by being a wuss.) Then she looks down and sees her bug-splattered self for the first time.

And totally freaks out.

She leaps off the handlebars and jumps. And twitches. And flicks. And runs around in circles. The whole time, she's singing, *"GLO! OH-OH-OH! OH-OH-OH! RIA!"* which I translate into *Get them off me! Get them off me! GET THEM OFF ME!*

When I try to slap the bugs off her, she starts slapping me back. *Ow!* I step away and fall into the flower bed while Paige runs around in circles and swats at herself. She's lost it. I've got to do something!

So . . . I spray her full in the face with icy cold water from the garden hose.

I'm not trying to be mean or anything, I'm just trying to help her stop freaking out. And it seems to work. She quits running around and stands as still as a statue. I spray her for a little while longer and get most of the bugs off.

Paige stands there, shocked and shivering. I wave my hand in front of her eyes. Nothing. She has brain freeze. "Paige? Talk to me. Or sing something."

She just stares and shivers some more, so cold her lips are blue. I've got to get her inside and warmed up.

But the front door's locked. "Do you have the key?" I ask. She reaches into her pocket with one shivering hand. She pulls out a key and then drops it. "I'll do it," I say.

I open the door and Paige walks inside with a slow, miserable, Frankenstein lurch. I start to follow her in—and so does the moped, which wiggles like a friendly dog. "You wait in the bushes till I come back," I tell it, feeling stupid. Like a moped's going to understand what I'm saying. But this one does. It droops a little sadly as it putt-putts into the bushes next to the house and parks.

CHAPTER

20

As I follow a cold and soggy Paige into the living room, I take a look around. This place couldn't be less like my house. My house is shabby and cluttered, and there are photos everywhere: me and Madison, from age one minute to last week; my parents with funny haircuts; my grandparents with funny haircuts; my uncles with no hair at all; family pets; family cars; family everything.

But Paige's house looks like no one really lives here. The living room is as new and clean as the pictures in the decorating magazines my mom reads.

Paige zombie-walks down a hallway into a bathroom, goes into the shower stall without bothering to undress, and turns the hot water on full blast. Her blue lips start to turn pink again.

"I'll go get you some clothes," I say.

She shakes her head no.

"I don't mind at all."

I go back into the hall and start opening doors. The first one leads to a home office with a lot of very fancy diplomas on the wall. Wow. Paige's father is a doctor from Stanford University School of Medicine. *That's* why they can afford such a nice lawn.

I open another door. Just a closet.

I open *another* door. And I'm instantly confused. It's a kid's room, but it can't be Paige's. There's a chess set. Science-fair trophies. A planet mobile. A bookcase full of Nancy Drew mysteries and Baby-Sitters Club books. This is the bedroom of a geeky kid. I pick up one of the trophies and read the plaque at the bottom: *First Place, Fourth Grade Science Fair—Paige Harrington.*

For the second time in a week, I gasp. This is more shocking than Sunny's bangs. Maybe even more shocking than finding out that fairy godmothers are real.

Paige Harrington, the most popular girl in the universe, *is a secret geek!*

Paige suddenly appears at my side, wearing a bathrobe and looking furious. She tries to grab the trophy out of my hand, but I'm too fast for her. I have a five-year-old sister. I've got moves.

"You are so busted," I say. "I bet at your old school you were smart and not popular. And then you came here and faked it!"

Paige grabs a pad of Post-its and scribbles: *Tell anyone, and I'll kill you.*

I check the room out some more. "You don't need a fairy godmother. You've gone from geek to chic all by yourself!"

Some of the anger fades from Paige's face. Then she writes, *I want to sing!*

"I know, I know. I'm working on it! But couldn't you have picked something easier?"

Paige writes, *I sound good in the shower.*

I can't help laughing, and then I worry that I've hurt her feelings. But Paige smiles a little. For the first time since I've met her, she doesn't seem like Miss Perfect. She seems human.

Paige writes, *Do you really think you can make me a good singer?*

"You want me to be honest?"

Paige nods.

"I'm not sure, but I'll do the very best I can. We need to work together. What do you say?"

Paige grins and points at her throat.

"Sorry. I forgot," I reply.

She reaches over and shakes my hand. I guess that means we're working together.

Suddenly, there's a voice from the living room: "Paige! I'm home!"

"Your dad?" I whisper, and Paige nods.

A moment later, Paige's dad comes into the room. He would

be handsome if he didn't look so exhausted. I don't want him to find out about the angel-singing problem, so I wave. "Hi, Dr. Harrington! How are you?"

He gives me a tired glance. "I've been covering shifts at the hospital for over thirty hours. How do you think I am? I'm going to bed. You can come back and visit some other time."

But I need to plan things out with Paige, so I wing it. "Would it be all right if Paige came over to my house for a sleepover tonight?"

Paige looks surprised, but then she gives her dad a thumbs-up.

Dr. Harrington asks me, "Are your parents all right with this?"

"Sure! It was their idea! They say a house isn't a home without a sleepover." Paige gives me a kick. I guess that *was* a little much.

Dr. Harrington seems too worn out to notice. "Fine. Make

sure to leave contact numbers with my answering service." He turns and leaves the room.

I can't believe how easy that was. No matter how tired they were, my parents would have smelled something fishy. But Paige doesn't seem at all surprised; she starts putting clothes in her backpack.

I suddenly think of something: "Do we need to ask your mom, too?"

Paige shakes her head and keeps packing.

CHAPTER

21

We walk out the front door, and Paige leaps back, terrified, when the bushes rustle and the moped rolls up to us. I have to admit it was a pretty wild ride for her, being a windshield and all.

I say to the moped, "Can you take us home? No going up walls or through stores. And you've gotta go slow." I swear it looks disappointed, but it gives a couple of short beeps that seem to mean yes. So I get on the seat, and Paige hesitantly climbs on behind me.

When we arrive at my house, I'm surprised to see Sunny waiting on the porch. Her mouth drops open as the moped pulls up and we get off.

She looks at me, hurt and angry: "So *this* is why you've been ditching me? You moped-riding double-crosser!"

I say, "It's not what it looks like."

"Really? 'Cause it *looks* like you're out having fun with your new best friend and not even caring how I feel!"

"That's not it." Now that Sunny's talking to me again, I can finally tell her the truth. So I take a deep breath and say, "I accidentally hurt Paige's fairy godmother. So now *I* have to be Paige's fairy godmother. And this moped is really an apple core. I can do magic!"

Sunny looks even more hurt. "You *liar!*" She stomps away. I don't know what I was expecting. Paige didn't believe it, either, at least not till the moped.

The moped!

I say, "Moped, fetch Sunny!" It waggles happily and zips off.

Sunny sees the driverless moped roaring up to her and SHRIEKS. She runs, and the moped chases her like a friendly red dog going after a stick.

Finally, the moped bumps her from behind, tosses her onto its seat, and zooms her back to the porch.

Shocked speechless, she looks at it, at me, and at Paige.

Paige pats Sunny's shoulder sympathetically and sings, *"GLO! OH-OH-OH! OH-OH-OH! RIA!"* which clearly means *I totally understand what you're going through.*

Sunny finally finds some words: "Lacey, you're telling the truth! You *can* do magic!"

"Yes!"

She gives me a hug, back to her old self.

"We're having a sleepover," I say. "You want to ask your mom if you can stay?"

Since it's a school night, Mom and Dad take a little convincing about the girls' staying over, but when we promise to be in bed by ten, they're okay with it. They're curious about Paige and start peppering her with questions, so I tell them she can't talk because she's strained her voice from two hours of cheerleading practice and three hours of play practice.

Paige, Sunny, and I go to my room. And with Paige texting and me talking, we get Sunny up to date on what's been happening. This is a lot of work, so we decide to wait till midnight, when Paige's voice comes back, before making any more plans.

It doesn't take long for Mom, worried about Paige's throat, to come in with tea and lemon. Dad's worried, too, so he brings her a scarf. And a moment later, Madison shows up with a story-book, insisting, "This is a special book for sore throats." It's actually *Barbie Princess Playtime*, but Madison likes any excuse to read it.

I roll my eyes at Paige to show that I know how weird my family is and that she doesn't have to pay any attention. But Paige smiles like she doesn't think they're weird at all.

———

We're pretending to be asleep in my bedroom when the clock hits midnight, which is when my angel spell should wear off. Sunny and I both look at Paige. "Say something!" Sunny says.

To my extreme relief, Paige can talk again. The first words out of her mouth are: "I just want to know one thing. . . ."

"How we're going to fix your voice?" I ask.

"No, not that." Paige turns to Sunny. "What did you do to your bangs? They look *terrible*!"

"Lacey was supposed to come with me, but I had to go to the salon on my own!"

"She didn't go with you? Everyone knows you have to have a spotter when you get your bangs cut. Or else . . ."

". . . they turn out like this."

Paige says, "Lacey! How could you do that?"

"*I had wand lessons!*"

"So, use your wand to fix Sunny's bangs!"

"They'd only be fixed till midnight, and I'd have to do it every day."

Sunny says, "I'm okay with that. Fix my bangs!"

I'm a little tempted. Sunny's hair does look bad. "I could try, but what if I just make them worse?"

Sunny says, "They couldn't be worse!"

"You could be bald. Or you could have snakes for hair."

She covers her hair with her hands. "That couldn't happen, could it?"

"It wouldn't be on purpose. But I didn't make Paige sing like an angel on purpose, either. Anyway, we have to stop talking about bangs and start talking about making Paige's dream come true. There's the Ann Estey problem—"

My bedroom door suddenly opens, and Mom comes in, wearing a bathrobe. "Girls! Less talking, more sleeping! Go to bed!"

I dive into bed, and Sunny and Paige scramble into their sleeping bags on the floor. "Good night, Mom!" I say. "Good night, Mrs. Unger-Ware," Sunny and Paige both say.

Mom looks at Paige. "Your voice is better! I knew honey and lemon would do the trick." She turns out the light. "Good night, girls. Sleep tight. Don't let the bedbugs bite." And she closes the door behind her.

Turning on my flashlight, I notice a funny expression on Paige's face. I tell her, "We don't really have bedbugs. She just says that."

Paige nods. "I know. My mom used to say that."

Sunny pats her on the shoulder. "Did your folks split up? My dad lives in Vancouver now."

"No. My mom died last year."

Oh. I didn't know that, and I'm sure Sunny didn't, either. Sunny puts her hand out to pat Paige on the shoulder again, but stops herself and folds her hands in her lap. A pat's not enough; nothing would be enough. There's a long silence in the room.

Finally, I say, "What was she like? Your mom, I mean."

"She was amazing! So pretty . . . Everybody said so. And she was good at everything and had a million friends. Nothing like me."

Sunny is shocked. "What are you talking about? That's *exactly* like you!"

"No, it isn't. Mom was special. She would have gotten the lead in *Cinderella* without even trying. *I* want to be special."

I think about the way Paige has transformed herself from science geek into cheerleader—and how much she wants to be in the play now. She wants to be like her mom!

Before I have a chance to ask more questions, Paige changes the subject. "So what are we going to do about Ann Estey?"

Sunny asks me, giggling, "Why don't you turn her into a frog?"

"Not so loud," I say.

Sunny whispers, "If Ann's a frog, she can't be in the play, and Paige can get the part."

I whisper back, "But that's so not fair. She's really good, and she's really excited about it."

Sunny says, "They can't both be Cinderella."

"I know! That's the problem! But I don't want to do something bad to Ann."

Paige's eyes light up. "So, do something good to her."

Sunny and I look at her questioningly.

Paige explains, "Being Cinderella's good, but there's gotta be something better. You could make Ann a movie star."

Sunny nods. "Or get her a trip to Paris!"

But I already see problems: "I don't think I'm a good enough fairy godmother to do any of that. I know I could make her a dress out of paper towels, but the rest sounds pretty hard."

Sunny hasn't heard this part before. "Really? You can make dresses?"

"Only ugly ones. Spells are tough. I could try to make her a star, but what if she turns into a real star? You know, a gigantic burning ball of hot gas . . ."

Sunny grins. "You mean, turn her into Mr. Griffith?"

Paige and I can't help snickering, but this is no time for jokes. I say, "I could send her to Paris, but there's a Paris in Texas and probably a million other ones."

Paige says, "Well, you just need to be really, really, really specific."

"I tried to do that with your voice. And you sang 'Gloria' all day. The spells need to rhyme, too. Like 'For a change you'll sing like an angel.'"

Paige shrieks and covers her mouth, but I smile. "Don't worry. It doesn't work without the wand."

Paige slumps in relief, but Sunny just asks me, "*Why* do they need to rhyme?"

"It's just a rule, like stopping at a stop sign or . . . never getting your bangs cut without a spotter."

We all sit there, thinking. It would be a lot easier to turn Ann into a frog.

Sunny's the first to come up with something: *"Don't* be really, really specific. Be vague! What about 'Give Paige the part, but don't break Ann's heart'?"

"That's pretty good," I say.

Paige looks at Sunny, impressed. "That's *really* good."

We decide that first thing tomorrow, that's exactly the spell we'll use.

Just as I start to fall asleep, Paige whispers, "Lacey?"

"Yeah?"

"I'm sorry I called you Underwear Girl."

"It's okay. I'm used to it."

"But I'm still sorry."

I never thought I'd hear those words coming from Paige Harrington's mouth.

CHAPTER
22

At six the next morning, Mom stumbles into the kitchen and sees the three of us already dressed and eating cereal. "What are you doing up?"

I say, "We've got play rehearsal!"

"This early?"

"There's a lot to do!"

I'll be so glad when my lying days are over.

I remember something as we're going out the door. I run to my room and put Katarina's cocoon in my pocket. She might as well come with me.

As Paige, Sunny, and I walk over to Ann's, Sunny says, "Can you just aim the wand at her house?"

"No," I say. "I've got to be looking right at her."

Paige looks at me with sudden understanding. "So that's why you were following me yesterday at school?"

I nod.

"I thought you were just being weird."

"You can't get much weirder than being a fairy godmother."

When we reach Ann's house, Paige says, "What do we do now?"

"Wait here till she comes out."

Sunny says, "We could just knock on the door."

"What if it's her mom? I can't exactly tell her, 'Hi! We're here to put a spell on your daughter!'"

"Good point," Sunny says.

"So we wait."

We sit on the curb and stare at Ann's front door. After a while, Sunny asks Paige, "How did you do it?"

"Do what?"

"Get so popular so fast."

Paige thinks about it. "It's easy, you just take everything you like . . . and stop doing it."

"But that doesn't sound like any fun," Sunny says.

"Who said being popular was fun?"

"So why try?"

Paige says, "If you're not popular, you're nobody."

Sunny shakes her head. "If you're not popular, you still matter!"

Paige doesn't look convinced.

Then a faint sound of singing drifts out of the house. *"I lost my shoe and you. . . ."*

"It's Ann!" I say. "Where's that coming from?"

We walk down the driveway, listening. And sure enough, we see Ann's head through the bathroom window. As the singing continues, Paige sighs. "I could never be that good."

I've got a straight shot at Ann, or at least her head. I toss the spell and chant, "Give Paige the part, but don't break Ann's heart."

Ann keeps shower-singing without missing a note.

"Nothing happened," Sunny says.

She's right. Nothing has happened at all.

Then:

There's a SCRREEEEECCHHH of tires, and a delivery truck barrels around the corner on two wheels—and heads right for us!

"Watch out!" I yell. We all dive out of the way as the truck roars past us.

CRUNCHHHHH! The truck smashes into the oak tree in Ann's front yard. An instant later, the truck's back door pops open and hundreds of plastic jars fly out like cannonballs.

We have to duck and dive to stop from getting hit in the head. It's like dodgeball times a hundred.

As the jars fly by, Sunny grabs one. It has a label showing

a smiling old guy in a green cowboy hat. She says, "It's Abner's Pickles. I *love* Abner's Pickles." She pulls one out and takes a bite.

Paige stares at the street full of bouncing jars and asks me, "Did you do this?"

"No. You heard the spell. I never said one word about pickles."

"Maybe you were thinking about them when you said it," Sunny says.

"I was not thinking about them!"

The truck driver stumbles out in a daze. "I kept pumping the brakes and pumping the brakes! But then, *tree*! Blammo! Pickles!"

Paige looks at me, appalled. "You *did* do this."

The spell was supposed to be so simple nothing could go wrong. And look what happened.

Suddenly, a news chopper hovers above us. A moment later, news vans from channels Two, Five, and 56, the Spanish station, pull up in front of the house. Reporters and cameramen jump out of the vans and start filming.

Sunny says, "All this for one smashed pickle truck?"

I say, "Maybe they *are* here by magic. But what does this have to do with Ann?"

The reporters face the cameras as if the spilled pickles were the biggest story ever.

Channel Two reporter: "It was raining pickles here on Parkdale Street. . . ."

Channel Five reporter: "This is Ralph Render reporting live from the site of the great pickle calamity. . . ."

Channel 56 reporter: *"La tranquilidad de la mañana fue rota por el ruido de la caída de los pepinillos. . . ."*

When the guy from Channel Two sees me, Sunny, and Paige standing near the house, he hurries up to us with his microphone. "Here, with a Channel Two exclusive, are three eyewitnesses to the disaster. Girls, tell the viewers what you saw!"

I'm going to be in such big trouble!

I'm about to say how sorry I am when Paige jumps in. "We didn't see a thing. Not one thing."

Sunny adds, "Magic had nothing to do with this at all. Besides, there's no such thing as magic."

And I say, completely truthfully, "I don't know what happened."

The reporter stares at us, disappointed. Suddenly, there's a voice behind us. *"I* saw the whole thing!"

It's Ann Estey. She's gotten dressed and looks prettier than I've ever seen her—as if she planned to be on TV. She's got makeup on, and even though her hair is damp from the shower, it's pulled back neatly with a tortoiseshell clip.

All three reporters jam their microphones in her face.

"What did you see?"

"What were you doing when the accident happened?"

"¿Estabas asustada por los pepinillos?"

Ann faces the reporters like she's been waiting for this on-camera moment all her life. She says, "I was so scared! I was sure it was an earthquake. My first thoughts were for my parents and my dear little dog, Binky. I am so grateful we are all safe."

There's the sound of a siren, and one of the reporters says, "The police chief's here!"

Oh, geez! The police chief!

When the reporters start to move toward the approaching car, Ann reaches out and grabs the Channel Five microphone. "I wanted to mention, if there are any talent scouts in the TV audience, that I will be appearing onstage this Saturday night as Cinderella in *Cinderella, the Rock Opera.*"

The Channel Five reporter tries to yank the microphone from her, but Ann won't let go. She sings in a loud, clear, pretty—and totally inappropriate—voice, *"I lost my shoe and you! I can't believe it's true! I don't know what to do!"*

The reporter finally grabs the microphone back and walks away. Ann watches him go like a Miss America contestant who's just blown the talent competition.

Weird. Pickles, reporters, and the police chief. Maybe a vague spell wasn't such a good idea.

CHAPTER

23

As we walk toward school, Paige says, "Don't feel bad, Lacey. You tried."

Why did she have to be nice? If Paige had been the snotty person I thought she was, being a fairy-godmother failure would have been way easier.

"It's only Wednesday. We've got plenty of time to get you your dream," I tell Paige, trying to sound sure, but feeling really worried.

I don't fool Sunny, because she gives me a quick hug and says, "I'll help you come up with a new spell in homeroom."

It might work. I always get a lot done in homeroom. I wrote half my zoo essay there, didn't I?

OMG!

The zoo! The interview's today! I've been so busy with Paige that I forgot all about it. Those animals are going to eat me alive—for real. I have to get out of it! I just need a little time to think . . .

. . . which I don't get. When we turn the corner near the school, Principal Nazarino stands right by the front door. I take a deep breath and tell myself it's just a coincidence.

Except it's not. Principal Nazarino says, "There you are, Lacey! The zoo people just called. Your interview's at nine." She reaches over and straightens my collar. "Don't slouch! You know how important this is!"

I say, "I forgot to tell my mom. And I don't have a ride. Please, can't we change it to next week?"

"Don't be ridiculous. I'll phone your mother and get permission, and I'll drive you myself. Problem solved." Pulling out her cell phone, she snaps at Paige and Sunny: "Don't stand there staring, girls! Get to class!"

Sunny and Paige don't have a choice. They walk away.

I call to them, "See you at lunch!"

Unless the polar bears eat me first.

Principal Nazarino tells me, "You stay here. I'll bring the car around."

As I wait for Principal Nazarino on the steps, I unzip my jacket pocket and look at the cocoon. There's not a crack or even a smudge on its shiny surface. One of the nail-polish companies should find out what it's made of and bottle it.

Zipping the cocoon back inside my pocket, I know I'm on my own.

———

We park in front of the zoo, where a woman is waiting at the curb. Principal Nazarino tells me, "Don't mess this up."

There's only one other thing I can do: play the barf card. Clutching my stomach, I say, "I don't feel too good! It must be the Tortilla Surprise my dad made last night."

"You'll be fine. Go! I've got a parent meeting, so I'll be back in an hour."

I could drop dead, and Principal Nazarino would still make me do this interview. So I hop out of the car, and she speeds away.

The friendly-looking woman from the zoo shakes my hand. "Hi, there! I'm Marybeth, the director's assistant. You must be Lacey," she says. "We all liked your essay."

"Thanks."

"The director is waiting for you in his office. It's just past the gorilla habitat."

As we walk toward the stone pillars of the entrance gate, we hear the usual noisy zoo sounds of animals snorting and squawking. But the very instant I walk through the gate, there's complete silence.

Scary silence, as if the animals know I've arrived and are watching my every move.

Marybeth doesn't notice, and I tell myself even zoos have to be quiet once in a while.

We walk through the African habitat, where elephants, hippos, lions, and giraffes all glare at me like they're Bambi and

I just shot their mother. I stop in my tracks—they hate me.

Marybeth says, "I know it's kind of a hike, but we're halfway there. You can see the director's office at the top of the hill."

Oh, geez. We're only halfway there.

Oh, *geez*. The hippo's getting up.

I've been to the zoo a million times, and I've barely even seen the hippo move. When she's feeling super energetic, she wiggles her ears to stop the birds from landing on her head, but that's it. Now she lumbers over to the pond near the fence and looks me straight in the eye for a second, just to make sure I know this is for me. And then she belly-flops into the mud, splashing dirty water right in my direction. I jump back.

Marybeth looks at the hippo, surprised. "Zenobia's lively today!"

Across the path, the hyenas stand in their pen and laugh at me.

I hurry toward the office, and Marybeth has to jog to keep up. We go past the gorillas, who are behind their moat and fence. Maybe they won't notice me; after all, they must have plenty of gorilla things to do.

They notice me, all right—when I walk by, they go crazy. As the gorillas beat their chests and roar, Marybeth stops and stares. "What's gotten into them?"

Getting more and more excited, the gorillas fling themselves at the fence. It's high and strong, but I bet they could get over it if they wanted to. And they really seem to want to. I call over my shoulder, "Last one to the director's office is a big gorilla!"

And I run like my life depends on it, which it may.

The zoo director is scary, like a combination school principal and dentist. He sits behind his big desk and fires off questions, about me, my school, my feelings about the current state of world wildlife, and how I would "best allocate scarce zoo resources."

He knows I'm twelve, right?

Then he asks me to explain my theories about modern zoo management in today's society.

Nope, he thinks I'm thirty with a Ph.D. in zoology.

He puts on a pair of those funny half-glasses and flips through my essay. "I was especially interested in your suggestion about doing a baby giraffe exhibit. You seem to know a lot about them."

I remember what Sunny told me and say, "Did you know that people used to call them camelopards because they looked like camels with leopard spots?"

"Yes, I did," he says over the top of his glasses.

Oh. This might be bad. Maybe I just insulted his intelligence. Adults can be very touchy when you do that.

"But I didn't learn that until I was in college. You're a bright girl." He takes off his glasses and smiles at me. "I shouldn't be saying this, but you're by far our best candidate for zoo intern."

Thank you, Sunny, for giving me that college-level bit of trivia! And take that, Harry S. Truman Middle School!

The zoo director stands up and says, "Good job, Lacey. I'm sure I'll be seeing you soon."

As he leads me out of the office, all I can think is: *Yay! We're done! I did it!*

Marybeth is waiting outside the door. "Ready for the tour, Lacey?" she asks.

Tour? What tour? Marybeth sees my blank look and tells me, "You didn't think all you got to do this morning was a boring old interview, did you? Now comes the fun part. It's feeding time at the petting zoo, and you get to help."

Shoot! Just when I thought I was done here, they throw me into the petting zoo.

How can I get out of this? I run through excuses in my head: *I have a math test in half an hour; I need to get back to the yodeling competition; Bigfoot and I are having lunch.* And then I take a couple of deep breaths and calm myself down. It's the petting zoo, not the lion habitat. They pick these animals because there's no way they'll hurt little kids.

So I smile at Marybeth and say, "Let's go!"

CHAPTER 24

Marybeth and I walk up a steep hill and go through a gate into the petting zoo. She points at the animals waiting patiently by their feed troughs and says, "The petting zoo doesn't open till eleven. So you'll get a little one-on-one time with the gang."

I'm worried that the animals aren't tied up, but I keep reminding myself that they're friendly. In fact, I know most of them from when I was little. Gus, the shaggy pony. Two goats named Lewis and Clark (Lewis is a girl). Curly, the sheep. Lulubelle, the potbellied pig. And some rabbits and baby chicks in an open-topped pen. It's about as scary as *Pat the Bunny*.

A guy wearing blue coveralls comes out of the stable with buckets of oats. Marybeth says, "Lacey, this is Raymond, who takes care of the animals here in the petting zoo. You two will be working together if you get selected."

Raymond smiles at me. Instead of shaking hands, he gives me a bucket. "Gus is waiting for you."

I take the bucket over to the pony. "Here's your breakfast!" I say, way too enthusiastically. As I get close, Gus flares his nostrils like I smell bad. I pour the oats into the trough and step back fast. He's not a big pony, but he has awfully big teeth. Gus sniffs the food but doesn't take a bite.

"Yummy, yummy! Good oats," I say, feeling kind of stupid.

When Gus trots away without eating, Raymond looks confused. "He's never turned down a meal in his life! I wonder if he's sick."

He's not sick. It's me.

And Gus isn't the only one. Instead of paying attention to their food, the other animals stare at me. Even Marybeth notices. "And what's wrong with *them*, Raymond?"

"They were fine a minute ago."

Suddenly Lewis bounds over and butts me in the knee with her hard little head. "Ow!" I say. She bleats as if she's warning every animal in the zoo that there's a maniac on the loose.

And the other animals in the zoo hear her, because from outside the petting-zoo fence comes the sound of roars and growls and squawks. I can't believe how loud they are.

A scared-looking staff member appears at the gate and calls to Raymond and Marybeth, "The animals are going crazy! We need your help!"

Marybeth tells me, "You stay here." Then she and Raymond run out the gate.

The second they're gone . . .

. . . I'm attacked on all sides by the petting-zoo animals.

Gus kicks out with a back leg; Lulubelle bites my pants cuff; Lewis and Clark butt my stomach.

And Curly *baas*.

I know that a *baa* doesn't usually sound scary, but the way Curly does it, it makes my blood run cold. He comes closer and closer. *Baa. Baa. Baaaaa!* Sheep are vegetarians, but I think he's planning to make an exception for me.

I back away from him and fall into the pen of bunnies and chicks. I lay there for a moment, the breath knocked right out of me. At least bunnies and chicks are harmless.

And then the chicks peck my hands. Ow! And the bunnies thump my head with their big bunny paws. Thump! Ow! Thump! Ow! Thump! Ow! They're the sweetest, softest things in the universe—and they, too, hate my guts.

I'm about to scream, "Help! I'm being attacked by bunnies and chicks!" But how lame is that? The petting-zoo animals don't care about all my hard work with Paige, they want me *gone*.

You'd think by now animals would only hate me partway. But no, they still hate me . . . all the way.

As the other animals come closer, I get up and scramble toward the gate, but they corner me next to the big metal feed cans. I grab a can lid like a shield and say in my bossiest voice, "Everybody, calm down and back away."

Instead, they all lunge for me at once.

To escape, I dive into an empty feed can and pull the lid closed over me. It's pitch dark in here and so dusty from oats that I can't help sneezing. But it seems pretty safe.

And then there's a loud *POW!* from Gus, kicking the side of the can; it tips over.

There's another kick against the side of the can, and I start to roll like I'm inside a clothes dryer. *Kawhump! Kawhump! Kawhump!* I brace myself as I tumble over and over and over.

I know I have to stop soon—there's a fence all around the petting zoo.

Then there's a *CRASH*! I could be wrong, but I think that that was the sound of me bursting through the petting-zoo fence.

Kawhump! Kawhump! Kawhump!

I *did* crash through the fence, and now I'm rolling down the steep hill that leads to the rest of the zoo. I go faster and faster. It's not a clothes dryer, it's a washer going into its fastest spin cycle.

Kawumpawumpawumpawumpawumpawumpawumpawump! As I brace myself against the inside of the can, with stiff arms and legs, I try to remember what's at the bottom of the hill. Is it the cotton-candy stand? That wouldn't be too bad to crash into. Is it the flamingo lake? That wouldn't be too bad, either—unless I can't get the lid off and I drown.

Kawumpawumpawumpawumpawumpawumpawu—
Silence.

I mean, dead silence. For a moment, the can spins out of control, but there's no sound from outside except a whoosh of air. It's like I've been launched into space in a rocket.

BAMMMMM!!!!!! I hit the ground again with a brain-joggling jolt and come to a stop.

When my head finally stops spinning, I reach up and push off the lid. Sunlight pours in, so bright I can't see a thing at first. I squint, trying to figure out what just happened. Let me see: I rolled down that big hill; I shot up that handicap ramp; I flew over that fence and moat.

Moat?

And landed in . . .

Oh no.

Oh no!

OH NO!

. . . the lion habitat!

Maybe they're still in their sleeping den?

My question is answered when a large, golden-brown eye peers into the can. Then that lion gets shoved out of the way and another lion peers in. And another. And another. It's snack time in lion land, and I'm the snack.

They stick their big paws into the feed can, and I shrink back, trying to make myself as small as possible.

Roaring and snarling, the lions push each other out of the way trying to reach me. I can't help it. I SCREAM and SCREAM and SCREAM some more.

And in the middle of all this snarling and screaming, I hear a cranky voice: "I will *not* be eaten by another cat. Where's the wand?"

I look down and see Katarina glaring up at me from just inside my pocket. She's burst out of her cocoon and still has shiny metallic pieces in her hair.

I've never been so happy to see anyone in my entire life.

"Katarina, you're back!" I say as we both dodge another lion's paw jabbing into the can.

"Give me the wand!"

The instant I pull the wand out of my pocket, Katarina yanks it away. Raising it above her head, she chants, "My head I shall keep, so lions go to sleep!"

She tosses the spell . . .

. . . and nothing happens. The lions keep roaring and circling the can.

(I just want to say here that I think wands are very unreliable. *Consumer Reports* should give them its lowest rating, even below SUVs that tip over when you turn too fast.)

Katarina tosses the spell again: "My head I shall keep, so lions go to sleep!" The lions just roar even louder.

Katarina looks at the wand, shocked. "Dear lord, it's bonded to *you* now, not me!"

The lions bat at the can like it's the world's biggest kitty toy. I brace myself and try to stay inside, but I get shaken out into the dirt, taking Katarina with me.

Every lion in the compound circles around us as Katarina shoves the wand into my hand and says, *"You* toss the spell! Toss it! Toss it!"

So I raise the wand over my head and chant, "My head I shall keep, so lions go to sleep!" I toss the spell just as the lions do that butt-shaking motion that means I'm going to be pounced on in about two seconds. (Julius does the same thing, remember?)

They make it halfway through the pounce and then, *kerthump!* Every single one of the lions falls asleep.

I collapse on the ground, still shaking with fear, but Katarina buzzes around my head like an angry wasp. "Give me that wand! It *can't* be bonded to you!"

I hand it over, and she lands on the head of a sleeping lion. She says, "Lion who's asleep, *baa* once like a sheep!" Remembering how scary Curly was, I cringe a little as she tosses the spell.

But just as before, nothing happens at all. She furiously hands the wand back to me. "You say it!"

So I raise the wand and say, "Lion who's asleep, *baa* once like a sheep!"

The lion opens his mouth and lets out a *baa* so loud that Katarina gets shaken right off his head. She lands in the dirt with a thump.

"Katarina! Are you all right?"

"No, I'm not all right! I'm horrible! Do you know what they call a fairy without a wand?"

"What?"

"UNEMPLOYED!"

She marches over and angrily kicks my foot.

"Stop that!" I say. "Why did this even happen?"

"It shouldn't have happened! I've cocooned before and never had a moment's problem with my wand afterward. Not a moment's!" Then she looks at me, crankier than ever—and that's saying a lot. "For the love of glitter, you didn't use my wand while I was cocooned, did you?"

"Um . . . just a couple of times."

"IDIOT! Now it won't re-bond with me unless Paige gets her dream. You silly girl! I cocoon for half an hour, and you can't keep your grubby hands off my wand?"

"Half an hour? It's been three days!"

Katarina is so shocked she stops kicking me and flies up to stare right in my eyes. "Are you serious? *Three days?*"

"Yes!"

As Katarina tries to wrap her head around this idea, I finally get a good look at her new, postcocoon self. Her wings are restored and more beautiful than they ever were; their colors are deeper, and there's a magical glow all around them. Her hair is red and silky. But her face is as cranky as ever—I guess cocooning can only do so much.

Trying to make her feel better, I say, "On the plus side, your wings look gorgeous!"

She ignores the compliment and flutters back down to the ground. She says, "I'm fresh out of a cocoon and all healed. But can I take over? Noooooooooo! My wand is bonded to you! A wand that I've used for four hundred and twenty-two years!"

"I'm sorry. I didn't do it on purpose."

"You don't do anything on purpose. Have you exploded Paige's head yet?"

"No. The only thing I exploded was a pickle truck."

Katarina lets out an angry hiss. "This is a nightmare! I want to go back to my cocoon!"

"Fine with me. I've been doing this all by myself for three days. I don't need you."

Katarina shouts, *"You don't need me?* One more second, and you would have been cat food!"

We glare at each other for a moment or two. I open my mouth to say something mean. The meanest thing ever.

But I stop myself. Katarina's right about the lions. And even with Sunny's help, I'm not sure I'm going to be able to fix Paige's voice by Saturday. I hate to say it, but I don't think I can do this without her.

So, instead of saying something mean, I say, "All right. I need you. But you need me, too."

"I do not!"

"Do, too! Unless you want to be a dryer fairy for the rest of your life!"

The anger slowly drains away from Katarina's face. She looks up and wags her finger at me. "I'm going to be watching you every step of the way. And no using the wand unless I tell you specifically what to do. I'm the professional here—you're only my assistant. One wrong move, girlie, and I'm leaving, dryer or no dryer! Do you understand me?"

"Yes!"

She flies down into my pocket and zips it up behind her. I guess this is the end of the discussion.

One of the lions rolls toward me, and I squeak like a frightened mouse, thinking he's waking up. But he just gives a luxuriant stretch and yawns, without even opening his eyes. I can't resist reaching over and petting him. This may be the only chance I get in my whole life to pet a lion. His mane is soft and golden, and the insides of his ears glow in the sunshine like pink seashells. This is *cool*.

Then I start hearing the other zoo animals bellowing and trumpeting angrily. There's a little voice from my pocket: "Leave that mangy lion alone and get us out of here!"

"How? We can't get out the way we came in."

"I know that. Say, 'I need to help Paige! Get me out of this cage!'"

"But—"

"Just use the wand and say it!"

Will that really work? There's only one way to find out. I chant, "I need to help Paige! Get me out of this cage!"

I gently float up over the moat and land on the path outside the habitat. "It worked!" I say.

"Of *course* it did."

Five minutes later, I'm outside the zoo, waiting at the curb with Katarina in my pocket. The animals are shrieking angrily inside, but none of them has gotten out. Good job, zoo architects!

Marybeth runs up. "There you are, Lacey! I was worried about you!"

"Principal Nazarino told me to wait for her here."

An elephant trumpets inside, and Marybeth says, "Crazy day, today!"

"I'm sure things will calm down soon." And I know that the second I leave, they will.

CHAPTER

25

When we drive back to the school, Principal Nazarino is furious to find a long green limousine parked in her reserved parking spot. She honks.

The doors to the school open and Ann Estey, her mother, and an old man in a green cowboy hat that matches the limousine walk out, followed by dozens of gawking kids.

Principal Nazarino says, "Who is that man?"

OMG! It's the Abner's Pickle guy! (I know this, because I just saw his face on a hundred bouncing jars.) What's going on?

Principal Nazarino gets out of the car to investigate. I'm about to follow, but then Paige runs up and motions for me to roll down the window. She says, "You *did* crash that pickle truck! Your spell worked!"

Katarina pokes her head out of my pocket. *"Her spell worked?"*

Then, seeing Paige, Katarina squeaks in a surprised little

voice: "Paige Harrington!" She straightens out her wings and says in a deeper, much more serious voice, "Greetings and salutations! I am your fairy godmother! Not every girl receives this boon; you are one of the lucky few!"

I get goose bumps. Now, *this* is how a fairy godmother is supposed to act. Simple dignity.

Then, *plop*! Katarina totally ruins the effect by falling out of my pocket onto the floor mat.

I pick her up and say, "Paige, meet Katarina. Katarina, meet Paige."

Paige is wide-eyed. "Your wings are so beautiful!"

All dignity again, Katarina gives her a little bow. "Why, thank you, my dear."

Sunny suddenly pokes her head in the car saying, "Ann is—" When she notices Katarina, she gets sidetracked and blurts out, "Holy cow! She looks like your crazy Aunt Ginny!" Every shred of Katarina's dignity disappears as she gives Sunny the stink-eye.

I try to steer the conversation back on track. "Sunny, what's going on with Ann?"

"The Abner's pickle guy saw her on the news this morning. He hired her to star in a commercial in Chicago this weekend."

Paige adds, "Ann's going to be a singing, dancing pickle on national TV! Your spell worked! I can have the part without breaking Ann's heart, because she's getting something she wants even more."

Katarina shakes her head. "She wants to be a dancing pickle? What is this world coming to?"

Ann, her mother, and Abner reach the limo, and the driver scurries around opening the doors. Mr. Griffith runs up to them, out of breath and crazy-eyed. "Ann, you can't leave! You are my Cinderella!"

Ann looks at him, a little guilty. "I'm sorry, Mr. Griffith!"

"You can't do this to me!"

"I have to! It's my big break!" Giving Abner a million-kilowatt smile, she says, "It's like you're my fairy godmother!"

Katarina snorts. "A fairy godmother would never be caught dead in that hat."

Ann's mother and Abner get into the green car, but Ann stands outside for a moment, looking back at the school and the curious kids. She waves a princessy wave at them and says, "Good-bye, everyone! I'll never forget you!"

We all watch as Ann is chauffeured away in Abner's limousine.

Mr. Griffith looks like he's about to cry, but then he straightens his shoulders and deliberately turns his back on the departing car. "I have an announcement to make. Miss Ann Estey will be leaving the cast of Cinderella, the Rock Opera because of creative differences. There's once again a marvelous opportunity for a talented, lucky girl at this school. A girl who could follow in the long tradition of replacement actresses rising to the occasion

and far surpassing the ungrateful thespian who so callously left the show in the lurch."

Everyone looks at Mr. Griffith, interested but confused. There were a lot of words there.

"Auditions will be held at noon in the music room. The role of a lifetime awaits!" And he marches back inside the school like there's an inspiring soundtrack playing that only he can hear.

This is my last chance to get Paige the part, and I'm not going to let her down. I look at the others and say, "Everybody, meet in the janitor's bathroom in five minutes!"

Making sure the bathroom door's locked, I say, "Okay, Katarina. What's the spell?"

When she doesn't reply, we all turn and see her perched in front of the bathroom mirror admiring herself and her new wings. "Not too shabby, if I do say so myself. I look divine!"

"Katarina, concentrate."

She pats her red hair and says, "Soooo shiny!"

"Katarina!"

She studies her face and smiles with delight. "I don't look a day over four hundred!"

All three of us girls shout, "KATARINA!"

"All right! All right! It's a simple spell."

Paige says, "You're not the one who sang like an angel all day."

Katarina rolls her eyes and sniffs, "Classic rookie mistake."

I say, "You were cocooned! I was doing the best I could!"

Katarina ignores me. "Paige, darling. You can't be that bad. Sing us a little something."

Paige hesitates.

Katarina encourages her: "Don't be shy. You're in a nonjudgmental, loving place here." Now it's my turn to roll my eyes.

Paige screeches, *"I lost my shoe and you! I can't believe it's true!"*

Katarina claps her hands over her ears and shouts, *"Wow!* You stink! More than stink! You *stink-ink-ink-ink-ink!"*

I say, "Katarina! You said 'nonjudgmental' and 'loving'!"

"I know! But she *stink-ink-ink-ink-inks!"*

Paige breaks down in tears, runs into a bathroom stall, and slams the door behind her.

I say to Katarina, "Now, look what you've done!"

Sunny whispers, "But she really *does* stink."

Paige says, "I CAN HEAR THAT!"

Sunny claps her hands over her mouth and lets out a muffled "sorry."

Pondering, Katarina paces back and forth on the steel shelf under the mirror. "With that voice . . . the spell needs to be more delicate than I thought."

Sunny can't stop herself from quoting her favorite movie.

She does her best Wicked Witch of the West impersonation, stretching the last word out into an evil cackle: "These things must be done *delicately.*"

I smile, but Katarina just looks mystified. She's obviously never seen *The Wizard of Oz*. When she's sure there aren't going to be any more crazy cackles from Sunny, she continues: "Paige should, sing good!"

I say, "I know she should sing good! But what's the spell!"

"That's it. The spell is, 'Paige should, sing good!'"

"'Sing good?' That's not even grammatically correct!"

Katarina turns back to the mirror, humming and fluffing up her hair.

Sunny and I exchange glances, not believing the spell could be so simple. (Or so stupid.) Sunny says, "*We* could have come up with that!"

Katarina says, "But you didn't, did you?"

I pull the wand out of my pocket. What do I have to lose?

Except my entire future happiness.

"Paige," I say. "Are you ready?"

There's a long pause as we all stare at the closed door of the bathroom stall. I tell Paige, "Don't make me zap your feet. If I hit a cockroach by mistake, the roach is going to be Cinderella in the play."

Katarina says, "That happened to Ernestina Snoop in the

1700s. Dryer fairy today. But the prince loved that cockroach till the end of his days."

I'm suddenly curious. "Would a Cinderella cockroach hate me like all the rest of the animals?"

"No. As long as the spell lasts, the cockroach forgets it's an animal and thinks it's human."

Hmm . . . The next time pigeons are attacking, maybe I should try making them human. For a moment, I'm lost in thought; then Sunny tugs on my sleeve. "Earth to Lacey! You've got to help Paige!"

Sunny's right, so I tap on the the stall door. "Paige, please. Katarina is sorry she said you stink."

Katarina waggles her eyebrows and silently mouths, *Am not!*

I ignore her. "Paige, the only way you're going to not stink is if you come out of there and let me help you."

Just when I'm sure she's going to stay in that toilet stall for the rest of her life, the door finally opens. Paige says, "Okay. Help me."

CHAPTER

26

Cinderella wannabes cram the music room as Paige, Sunny, and I walk in.

Everyone is talking about Ann: "She's my best friend in the whole world!" "She's soooo talented!" "Someday I want to be a star just like her!"

Katarina whispers from my pocket, "Or at least a singing, dancing pickle."

Even Taylor and Makayla, who were too cool to audition the first time, now seem sure this could be their road to fame and fortune. Still in their cheerleader outfits, they wear so much glitter makeup it looks like they've fallen face-first into one of their own posters.

Mr. Griffith bustles in, all business. "Quiet, girls! Quiet!" Everybody looks at him expectantly. "Today is Wednesday. The play goes on at seven p.m. Saturday. And it must go on. That's barely three days. It sounds impossible, but I am up to the task. My question is, are you?"

The girls all eagerly nod, yes. It's like a bobble-head convention in here.

"Good! Let's begin." He sits down at the piano. "Please line up and be ready to sing the first verse of 'I Lost My Shoe and You.'"

The girls race to get in line. By the time all the pushing and shoving is done, Taylor and Makayla are in front, but Sunny and I have managed to elbow Paige into slot number three. (I'm pretty sure I saw Sunny pulling Isabelle Britt's hair, but I'm not going to think about that right now.)

Mr. Griffith tells the girls, "I appreciate your enthusiasm. Just remember to bring that, times a hundred, to the stage on Saturday. Taylor, you're first."

Taylor sprints up to the piano and gives Mr. Griffith her most dazzling smile. She says, "I want to tell you what a musical genius I think you are. All the songs are so very, very, very, very, very . . . *very*!"

Sunny whispers, "No wonder Taylor's flunking English."

Taylor bursts into song, very high and off-key. And I hear Katarina's muffled voice from my pocket: "Ye gods! She stinks, too!" Mr. Griffith obviously agrees. He stops playing and shakes his head like a dog with ear mites.

Makayla steps up and pushes Taylor out of the way. "My

turn!" she says, and Mr. Griffith starts to play again. Makayla screeches, *"I lost my shoe and—"*

"NEXT!" Mr. Griffith shouts. (From my pocket, I hear "STINKS!")

It's Paige's turn now, but when Mr. Griffith sees her, he puts up a hand, like a traffic cop. "Stop right there, Paige. As a singer, you make a wonderful dancing mouse."

There are snickers from the girls in the room. Paige looks crushed. I know Mr. Griffith is under a lot of pressure and everything, but he doesn't have to be so harsh. Besides, he loved her angel-singing, even if she did seem crazy.

"Next!" Mr. Griffith says, already turning to the line of girls.

I drag Paige up to the piano, saying, "That's not fair. These are new auditions. Paige deserves another chance."

"Absolutely not! We're on a schedule here!"

"But I've been coaching her. She's much better."

"I said no!"

Mr. Griffith stares at Paige and me like he wishes he could call security and have us dragged away. Then Paige sings: *"I lost my shoe and you. I can't believe it's true!"*

Everyone in the room listens to her in disbelief—good disbelief this time, because the spell has worked and Paige sounds fantastic. Like the spell says, she sounds *good*. Real good.

Mr. Griffith smiles in ecstasy. But there's a flicker of doubt in his eyes, as if he can't believe his own ears. "Sing the rest of the song, Paige."

She does.

He asks her to sing every other song in the score.

She does.

He asks her to sing "The Star-Spangled Banner."

She does, perfectly hitting those really high notes near the end that almost nobody gets right: *"and the land of the freeeeeeeeeeee."*

Mr. Griffith is about to have her sing every song ever written when the bell rings. He blinks his eyes like a man coming out of a wonderful dream. "Paige Harrington. Will you be my Cinderella?" he asks, literally going down on one knee.

The other girls in the music room slump in disappointment as Paige nods yes.

Nearly bursting with excitement, Sunny and I jump up and down and hug each other. There's a muffled voice from my pocket: "You're squishing me!"

Mr. Griffith claps his hands on our shoulders. "You girls certainly have a lot of energy."

"Sorry," I say.

"Let's see how much energy you have after you finish building my sets."

And just like that, Sunny and I are drafted for the stage crew of *Cinderella, the Rock Opera.*

CHAPTER
27

The next two days are a blur of rehearsals as Mr. Griffith works to get Paige up to speed. I thought all I would have to do was throw the spell every morning to change Paige's voice, but instead, Sunny and I are here hammering and painting and sewing and sweeping. All those lies I told my mom about working on the play have come true.

I beg Katarina to let me use some magic. What's the use of having a wand if you have to do all the work yourself? She says smugly, "No. It's not necessary, and it's not part of our deal."

She's found a safe spot up in the stage lights where she can watch without being seen. But once in a while she flits down to make fun of the way Chloe Martin is playing the fairy god-mother and to pester me about Paige's ball gown.

"It's supposed to be here any minute now," I say. "Mr. Griffith has a Broadway costume-designer friend who's making it. So we don't need to worry."

"You *always* need to worry about the dress."

"Not this time! It's under control!"

Katarina doesn't look convinced, but she flutters back up to the lights to keep her beady little eyes on things.

As Wednesday turns into Thursday turns into Friday, Sunny and I both feel like the "before" version of Cinderella. We're not dressed in rags, but Mr. Griffith yells at us so much he could be the evil stepmother. "Hammer faster! Paint faster! Sweep faster! And stop making so much noise!"

The only person he doesn't yell at is Paige. He listens to her magically beautiful voice, and his face glows like it's Christmas morning. Whole minutes go by without his screeching at anybody at all.

By Friday night, the play is looking pretty good. The dress isn't here yet, but the actors are all doing what they're supposed to be doing. The stepsisters are funny evil. The evil stepmother is evil evil. Chloe Martin as the fairy godmother is doing her best British accent. The mice are dancing with the proper amount of ennui. And Scott Dearden is being his charmingest Prince Charming.

All that's really left is for Paige and Scott Dearden to learn the choreography for their big waltz near the end. I'm not sure why there's a waltz in a rock opera. Isn't that pretty old-school for something that's supposed to be so cutting-edge? But maybe *Cinderella* has to have a waltz, just like *Rocky* has to have a fight and *Titanic* has to have an iceberg.

And right now, Scott Dearden is the iceberg that's about to sink the play. As a dancer, he's a really good football player. "No, no, no, NO!!!" Mr. Griffith shouts as Scott and Paige wobble across the stage. "Ow! Ow! Ow! OW!" Paige yelps as Scott stomps on her toes.

Mr. Griffith screams, "Scott, that's terrible! You're not playing football. You're trying to dance with her, not tackle her!"

So far, Scott has listened to all of Mr. Griffith's shouting and screaming without a single complaint. But he's finally had enough. He lets go of Paige and storms toward the exit door. "Fine! I quit!" *SLAM!*

The door closes behind him, and he's gone.

Mr. Griffith also storms off, shouting, "Everybody! Take five!" And *he* disappears into his office and slams the door behind him.

A moment ago, the play was in great shape. Now we don't have a Prince Charming or a director.

What a mess! I need to fix this somehow. So I tell the others, "I'll be right back!" and head for the exit door myself.

I find Scott unlocking his bike in the school parking lot. "You can't quit!" I say, so worried about the play I don't even notice his beautiful eyelashes. (But geez, they're long.)

"I already did."

"But you're great in the part."

"I suck. Everyone is gonna laugh at me."

I finger the wand in my pocket. It's an emergency, and Katarina's not here. Maybe I can figure out a spell that would work on him. But what if I make it so he can't do anything *but* dance? Scott won't be much use tomorrow if he dances his feet down to bloody stumps between now and midnight. Sure, it sounds like I'm exaggerating, but think about it. It could happen. And he's got such nice feet, too.

I'm not willing to risk bloody-stumpdom. But what else can I do? Scott's a football player, not a dancer.

I suddenly think of watching football with Dad and him shouting, "Look at that guy dance!" That gives me an idea, so I tell Scott, "Don't think of it as dancing. Think of it as football."

He looks at me, confused, and I say, "Football or dancing— it's all about blocking."

Now he's even more confused.

Grabbing both his hands, I say, "It's easier if I show you. I go to the left, you block on the left. I go to the right, you block me on the right. You want to keep me from making an end run around you." I wish Dad could hear me now. He would be so proud.

Scott stands there like a goalpost, so I start dragging him around the parking lot and chanting, "Go left, block left. Go right, block right," over and over again in a singsongy voice.

I expect him to push me away and take off on his bike any second, but I keep on chanting, "Go left, block left! Go right, block right!"

Just as I think this is hopeless, Scott gets it. Almost without his realizing it, his feet start moving in rhythm with mine.

In a whisper, Scott chants, "Go left, block left! Go right, block right!"

And just like that, we're dancing. We waltz around the parking lot in broad circles. I totally forget fairy godmothers and Cinderella rock operas and angry animals. I simply enjoy being here with Scott.

"You're a good teacher," Scott says, fluttering those long lashes at me.

And then it hits me! OMG! I'm dancing with Scott Dearden, the cutest boy in school!

I blush and go left when I should be going right. Our legs get all tangled up and we have to stop. "So? Ready to tackle the play?" I say, turning to go in.

"Thanks, Lacey. I always did think you were nice."

"You . . . thought about me?" I blurt out.

Now it's Scott's turn to blush.

I can't believe it! He thought about me! He thought about me!

We stare at each other for a moment. If this were a movie about my life, right now is where he would lean in and kiss me and the violins would start playing really loud.

But instead, SPLATTT!!!! A pigeon poops right on my head.

"Ewww!" I say.

"Ewww!" Scott says.

My life is *so* not a movie.

We hurry back inside.

———

By the time Mr. Griffith finally comes out of his office twenty minutes later, I've washed out the pigeon poop and pulled my hair back in a ponytail.

It turns out that Mr. Griffith has done some hairstyling, too. He's wearing an ugly black wig with bangs that flop down into his eyes. Not only that, he's dressed in a velvet tunic. And tights! Wow, that's something you can't un-see. Mr. Griffith says, "Nothing is going to stop this show, do you all hear me? *Cinderella* will go on tomorrow night if I have to play every part myself. Meet your new Prince Charming."

He finally gets the bangs out of his eyes, which now pop wide open—because on the stage in front of him, Paige and Scott are waltzing like they're finalists in a dance contest.

Mr. Griffith takes off the black wig, not bothering to hide his disappointment.

Katarina flies down onto my shoulder and hisses, "I told you, no discretionary magic."

I say, "It wasn't magic. It was football. So there."

It's past eight, and Mr. Griffith is still tweaking the play. He's got a million performance notes, none of them very important except to him. There are a dozen tired parents sitting in the back of the auditorium, including my mom. There's no way you could miss her. She's wearing one of the lime-green Hungry Moose T-shirts.

Finally, the janitor starts switching off lights, and the parents shoot to their feet to collect their kids. Mr. Griffith says, "All right! Everyone, be back here tomorrow at three p.m. sharp! I want to do one last run-through before the performance!"

My mom walks up to Mr. Griffith and says, "I have an idea." He looks at her suspiciously, as if she's about to tell him how to rewrite the play. But Mom continues, "My husband and I would be happy to bring dinner for everyone tomorrow. Something the kids will like."

Instead of saying, "Great! Fantastic!" like a normal person, Mr. Griffith shakes his head. "No junk food for my cast."

Mom is offended. "It wouldn't be junk food."

"No. I'll be providing high-protein shakes. Very nutritious. Meryl Streep swears by them."

"They're kids. They need more than a shake for dinner."

"No. Thank you!"

Mom glares at him as he turns and once again disappears into his office.

"What a rude man," Mom fumes as Sunny, Paige, and I (with a pocketful of Katarina) walk to the parking lot.

"Don't feel bad. He's like that with everyone," Sunny says.

"I'm not going to drink a drop of his high-protein shake," I tell her.

"Me, either!" Paige says.

"Me, either!" Sunny says, too.

Mom raises her fist in a mock salute: "Food solidarity! Who-rah!" Mom can be embarrassing sometimes.

We reach our car, and Paige says, "Well, good night, every-body!" and starts to walk away.

Mom asks her, "Isn't your dad going to pick you up?"

"No, he's working late at the hospital. It's no problem, I walk home all the time."

"Not tonight, you don't! Tonight you're coming to the Hungry Moose for Lasagnapalooza."

To my surprise, Paige says, "I'd love that." Lasagnapalooza isn't for everybody, and I've never seen a single cheerleader at the Hungry Moose. But I'm forgetting that Paige isn't an ordinary cheerleader. I bet her inner geek is starving.

Mom says, "Sunny, do you want—"

"Yes!" Sunny jumps into the car before Mom even finishes her sentence.

CHAPTER

28

It's an hour later, and Paige, Sunny, and I are each on our fourth helping of lasagna. We've got the restaurant's best table, the round one between the two mirrors that make it look like you're eating with smaller and smaller versions of yourself.

When Mom comes over and asks, "Who wants more?" we all groan. "That's the sound of satisfied customers!" she says.

In another corner of the restaurant, Xander, the waiter, carries a cake out to a woman who's eating with her family. He starts singing *"It's a Hungry Moose Happy Birthday!"* This is a song my mom and dad made up that always embarrasses me, but that the customers seem to like. Sure enough, the family sings right along with Xander.

I look at Paige, expecting her to be rolling her eyes. Instead, she watches the family a little sadly. "That seems like fun."

Sunny asks her, "What did you do for your birthday this year?"

"My dad had to work."

Mom frowns. "So you didn't do anything?"

"It's not like I'm a little kid. Birthdays aren't a big deal."

But Paige looks sad to me, and Mom notices it, too. She gives Paige's shoulder a squeeze as she goes back into the kitchen.

To change the subject, I look at the clock and tell Paige, "This time tomorrow night, you'll be getting a standing ovation for *Cinderella*." Then I ask her, "Is your dad coming to the play?"

She smiles. "Yes—he promised. I can't wait for him to hear me sing."

Sunny says, "If your dad's anything like my mom, he'll show up with eight cameras and a dozen roses."

"I don't care what he brings, as long as he's there," Paige says.

We talk for a while longer, and then the lights in the room suddenly dim. Mom, Dad, and Madison walk toward us with a big birthday cake glowing with candles.

Dad tells the customers, "We've got one more birthday tonight, folks. Paige here doesn't think birthdays are important, but we want to change her mind. Everybody, sing along!" Paige looks stunned.

"*It's a Hungry Moose Happy Birthday . . .*" Dad begins to sing, and we all join in. As the last words to the song ring out, Dad puts the cake down in front of Paige.

Paige whispers to Dad, "It's not my birthday!"

Dad whispers back, "It's belated."

Madison jumps up and down. "Blow out the candles! Blow out the candles!"

Paige smiles and takes a deep breath.

"Wait! Be sure to make a wish!" Mom says.

Paige thinks for a moment, makes a wish, and then blows out the candles on the cake. There's applause and whistling from the dining room.

Paige's eyes shine. "What a beautiful cake."

"I helped decorate it!" Madison says.

And the cake really is pretty. Big pink roses. Delicate green vines. And in the center, a plastic butterfly with beautiful wings.

Wait a minute. That's not a plastic butterfly—it's Katarina, who stands still as a statue, with a fake smile plastered on her face and a *Get me out of here, you idiot* look in her eyes.

Dad says, "Madison found the decoration. Doesn't it look like Aunt Ginny?"

Paige and Sunny, realizing that the butterfly is Katarina, start to giggle. Madison says, "She's really Lacey's hair clip. She tried to bite me, but I wouldn't let her."

"Good for you, honey," Mom says as she cuts the cake.

"The hair clip told me when she gets her wand back she's going to turn me into a toe. Why would she want to do that?"

"You're sure she didn't say, *toad*?" Sunny asks.

Madison loves this idea. *"Cool!"*

In my bathroom that night, it takes me forever to wash the dried icing out of Katarina's wings.

"I've never been so humiliated!" she sputters. "I came this close to getting my wings burned off!"

"But you didn't. We're almost done. One more night and you can fly away."

"Don't count your Cinderellas before they hatch."

"But you think we can do it, don't you?"

"We have to. You may enjoy the prospect of being an animal pariah, but I have no intention of ending up as a dryer fairy."

I'm not sure what a pariah is, but I don't like the sound of it. Then I tell myself we're doing good so far. What could go wrong?

CHAPTER 29

Saturday, the day of the play and the day of the full moon, starts out just fine.

Katarina and I go over to Paige's house with the wand, just like we did yesterday and the day before. I chant, "Paige should, sing good," and toss the spell at her. A gorgeous singing voice, no problem.

I don't know it yet, but this will be the last no-problem moment today.

We all stand near the stage watching Mr. Griffith open a big FedEx box—it's Cinderella's ball gown, straight from Broadway. He says, "Let me show you what a professional can do!"

Mr. Griffith reaches into the box and pulls out some crinkled, dirty-brown packing material. He rummages around in it, searching for the dress, but this is all there is. He speed-dials a number on his cell phone. "Hello, Deirdre? I just opened the package. I can't find the dress." He listens and turns pale. "This is it? It's so drab and brown. . . . It looks like a rock."

He's right. The dress, if that's what it is, looks exactly like a rock. A big, shapeless, brown rock with armholes.

Paige stares at the dress in disbelief. A moment ago she was so happy and excited. Now she looks like somebody just punched her in the stomach.

Mr. Griffith sputters, "Deirdre, I *know* I said rock opera! But it's still Cinderella! I don't care how conceptual it is, the dress can't look like a rock! You've got to whip something up and ship it to me before seven tonight!" He pulls the phone away from his ear and looks at it in disbelief. "Don't you hang up on me!" he shouts.

There's a voice from my pocket, so faint that only I can hear it: "I told you so. I told you so. I told you so."

I thought I'd seen Mr. Griffith have meltdowns before, but those were nothing compared to this. He grabs the rock costume and tries to rip it to bits. But it won't tear, not even a little. (Deirdre makes a really high-quality costume. Ugly, but high-quality.)

He throws the dress on the floor and stomps on it. The dirt from his shoes makes the dress look even more like a rock. Finally, he stands there panting and announces, "Listen, everybody. I'm sorry, but we cannot go on tonight. The play will be postponed till spring."

Spring! I can't wait till spring!

I blurt out, "NO! We *have* to go on tonight!"

Mr. Griffith looks at me sadly and says, "Oh, you remind me so of myself when I was young and my ideals had not yet been crushed. But we have to face facts." He looks down at the ugly dress on the floor: "No dress, no Cinderella. Everybody, go home."

And he drags himself into his office and shuts the door behind him. Again.

For a moment, we're all too shocked to say anything. Then Scott Dearden pulls on his jacket. "Well, you heard him. It's over." Everyone else starts talking at once.

I've got to do something. "Wait, everybody! Wait!"

Nobody pays any attention to me.

"Please, everybody! Wait!"

Then Sunny does one of her insanely loud whistles, the ones she saves for professional baseball games. Everyone shuts up—a lot of people even cover their ears. Sunny's that good.

This is my last chance. "The play is not postponed," I say. "I have a dress at home that will be perfect! Everybody, relax and drink a protein shake—I'll be back soon. Just don't let Mr. Griffith leave!"

"How are we supposed to do that?" Scott asks.

"Nail the door shut if you have to!"

So now, ten minutes later, Paige, Sunny, Katarina, and I are back in the janitor's bathroom. We're here so much we should start paying him rent.

I look for the paper-towel dispenser, but there isn't one, just one of those hot-air blowers. "Oh no!"

Sunny says, "What's the matter?"

"There's no paper towels! I need them to make the dress!"

Paige says, "You're joking."

When I run into the bathroom stall and come out with a streamer of toilet paper, Paige says, "*Please* tell me you're joking."

I say, far more confidently than I feel, "Fairy godmothers can make dresses out of anything. Katarina used to make dresses out of dirt! Beautiful dresses!"

Sunny and Paige look at Katarina, who's standing on the sink. I'm expecting a snide comment, but she just nods and says, "It was the Dark Ages. We were lucky to have dirt." Then she asks me, "You practiced while I was cocooned, right?"

Yeah, like I had time for that. "Of course I did," I lie. There's a hook on the back of the door, and I drape the toilet paper over it and step back.

Katarina asks, "And you remember the spell?"

"Yes, Katarina. 'Out of litter make a dress that glitters!' You made me say it fifty times."

This impresses Sunny. "You must be really good by now!"

I pull the little wand out of my pocket and raise it above my head. I've done so much other magic this week I'm sure I can do this. I chant, "Out of litter make a dress that glitters!" and toss the spell.

Poof! The toilet paper turns into . . . toilet paper. Fluffy toilet paper, but still, toilet paper.

I try it again. And again. And again. I do manage to make a couple of dresses, but they're all *ugly*. There's not a sparkle to be seen.

After a dozen more of these wardrobe malfunctions, Sunny holds one up. "The back is nice on this dress."

I grab it away from her. "That's the front."

Paige is about to cry, and I'm about to explode with frustration. I turn to Katarina. "Why can't I do this? I turned an apple core into a moped. I should be able to make one stupid Cinderella dress!"

"That's your problem: you think it's stupid. I've been saying it and saying it—the dress is absolutely crucial. And you've been ignoring me."

"I don't think it's stupid! I know the play can't go on without it!"

Katarina is getting frustrated, too. "Face it, you'll never be a good fairy godmother. You just don't have it in you."

Paige wipes her eyes and says, "Stop it! Lacey's a *great* fairy godmother. She even crashed a pickle truck for me."

Katarina says, "Hooray for her. But that doesn't help with the dress. We need a dress that sparkles! Shines! Glitters!"

I feel myself turning red. That's what's wrong with me—I don't have the glitter gene. I've come so far, but I won't be able to make a dress.

Because. I. Don't. Do. Glitter.

On the verge of tears myself, I run out of the bathroom.

CHAPTER
30

I run down the hall with the wand still in my hand. I just want to get away from them—from dresses, from friends I'm disappointing, from fairy godmothers who think I'm not good enough. I'm not going to cry. I'm not going to cry.

And actually, I'm *NOT* going to cry, because I'm mad! Boiling mad! Glitter is stupid! It's fake! It's pointless!

Storming down the hall, I mimic Katarina's raspy little voice, saying, "Out of litter make a dress that glitters!" and toss the spell. At a garbage can. At a poster. At a sneaker somebody dropped in a corner. *Zap! Zap! Zap!*

I hate glitter! I hate fake! I LIKE REAL! How did I ever get myself into all this? Oh, yeah . . . Katarina got trapped in some dumb glitter in my hair. *Glitter is evil!*

Zap! Zap! Zap! I'm so mad I toss the spell at everything I see.

I finally stop, in front of the stairwell window. Shouting about hating fake and liking real isn't going to do me any good. I'm not mad anymore, just sad that I'm such a failure. I am not going to cry. I am not going to cry!

I put my head in my hands and sob.

Sunny calls from the other end of the hall: "Lacey!"

"Go away!" I say without even bothering to raise my head.

"Look at what you did!"

"I know what I did. I made a big mess."

"No, *look*."

I'm getting mad again. I know I'm a failure! Why can't Sunny just leave me alone? I turn around, ready to tell her that.

And then I see what I've done.

Beautiful, glittery dresses float all up and down the hallway sparkling in brilliant colors. Green and red and blue, a gleaming dress for every *zap*. Sunny, Paige, and Katarina stare at the dresses in amazement. I do, too.

Paige walks from dress to dress, and every time she touches one, it spins and sparkles in the light. "How can I ever choose? They're all so beautiful!"

And they *are* beautiful. I say, "Wow! I did glitter!"

"I don't think so," Sunny says.

"What do you mean?"

"This isn't glitter. These are real."

"Real what?"

"Emeralds and rubies and sapphires." Sunny spins a dress

that's shining with white gems, and it catches the light like a billion fireflies. "I think this dress is covered with diamonds."

"Ooooh!" Katarina flies over to the dress.

"Ooooh!" Paige gently touches it. "This is my favorite!"

Sunny says, "There's gotta be thousands of real diamonds here."

I say, "There's no way those are real."

Sunny gathers up the hem of the dress and rubs it against the window, leaving behind tiny scratches. She looks at me smugly. "Only diamonds scratch glass like that. I saw it in a movie." She looks back at the dress again. "At least until midnight, this dress is worth about a zillion dollars. Lacey, you're good!"

"But how could that happen? I wasn't even thinking about the spell. I was just . . . *doing* it!"

Katarina tells me, "That means the spell came from your heart and not your head. What was in your heart?"

"I don't know! I was mad. I wanted things to be real, not fake."

Sunny points at all the jewel-covered dresses. "Well, that's what you got!"

Paige says, "I don't care if it's real or fake. It's the most wonderful dress I've ever seen!"

Katarina touches the diamond dress and smiles. "I do have to admit, this isn't half bad."

CHAPTER
31

The other kids are all twiddling their thumbs and drinking protein shakes when Paige makes a grand entrance into the auditorium. As she poses and twirls in the diamond dress, even the boys ooh and aah. It's funny the effect a zillion dollars' worth of diamonds has on people, even if they don't know they're real. With this dress, Paige's invisible spotlight is back on, shining as bright as the sun.

"Is Mr. Griffith still here?" I say.

Scott points toward Mr. Griffith's office.

"You didn't really nail him in, did you?"

"We didn't have to. He's been in there the whole time."

I go up to the office door, about to knock. Then I hear Mr. Griffith singing, *"I lost my shoe and you,"* in a slow, sad howl, like a country singer who's been run over by a truck.

Scott tells me, "He's been doing that since you've been gone. He's lost it!"

I knock on the door. "Mr. Griffith? It's Lacey. I found a dress."

More sad wailing from inside: *"I don't know what to dooooooooooo."*

"Mr. Griffith? It's going to be all right, really!"

"I can't believe it's truuuuuuuuuuuuuuuuue!"

"MR. GRIFFITH! PULL YOURSELF TOGETHER! WE'VE GOT A PLAY TO PUT ON!" I push the door open to find Mr. Griffith sitting at his desk, a big bag of Oreos in front of him, and his mouth encrusted with dark brown crumbs. He's not handling the whole canceling-the-play thing very well.

"Lacey, shut the door and go away!" he says, washing down several more Oreos with a big swig of protein shake.

But then he sees Paige in her diamond dress, and his mouth drops open, full of cookie goo. He leaps to his feet. *"Oooooooooh!"*

Suddenly all business, Mr. Griffith wipes the crumbs from his mouth and looks out at the kids. "What are you standing around gawking for? There's work to do! We've got a performance in three hours!"

Fifteen minutes before showtime, the play seems just about perfect. With a little luck, Paige will get her dream, and so will I.

I peek out through the curtain at the nearly full auditorium. My dad, my mom, and Madison are off to one side, and Sunny's mom is in the front row. (Sure enough, she's got eight cameras and a dozen roses, even though Sunny only helped with the sets. She's a good mom.)

The "orchestra" sits just below the stage. It's actually the Mellowtones trio from the Marriott Hotel, whom Mr. Griffith hired for the night.

Paige comes up behind me, wearing rags and artistically placed soot. "Do you see my dad?"

"Not yet. But it's so crowded I might have missed him."

Mr. Griffith strides out to the middle of the stage, clapping his hands for attention. "Circle 'round, everybody! We're about to embark on that most sacred of voyages, the one that takes place from curtain-up to final bows. The heart of every member of the audience is in your hands. And the thing that you must tell each one of them is—BLLEEEEAAAAAAHHHHHHHHH!!!!!!!!"

He throws up Oreos and protein shake all over the stage.

Gross!

Mr. Griffith's face is a weird shade of green. But he wipes his sweaty forehead and tries to continue. "I'm fine, I'm fine! And the show must go on!"

Then, BLEEAAHHHH!!! He throws up again. A moment later, he runs out of the auditorium, groaning.

I look at the other kids, and they're all green, too. Some are pale green. Some are purplish green. Scott Dearden is almost leaf green.

They clutch their stomachs and try not to look at the upchuck on the floor. Chloe Martin says, "I don't feel so good!" She covers her mouth with both hands and races out the emergency exit.

A moment later, there's a stampede as all the kids, cast and crew alike, follow Chloe out the door.

The only ones left onstage are me, Sunny, Paige, and Katarina, who crawls out of my pocket and sits on my shoulder.

"What just happened?" Sunny asks.

I suddenly remember the icky video my dad made us watch about food safety, and how it only takes a tiny bit of bacteria to make people really, really sick. I look at the mess on the floor and say: "Food poisoning. I bet anything it was the protein drink!"

Then the Mellowtones strike up the opening bars of the overture. The play can't start yet! The entire cast and crew are in the parking lot, puking! I've got to stall for time.

When I slip out through the curtain and stand at the front of the stage, there's applause, because people think the show has begun.

Madison jumps up and down in her seat, shouting, "That's my sister! Yay, Lacey!" She gets a laugh from the audience, and it takes a second or two for them to quiet down enough to hear what I'm saying.

"Ladies and gentlemen! Welcome to *Cinderella, the Rock Opera!* There will be a short delay before the show starts. But it won't be long, I promise!"

The Mellowtones stop playing and look at their watches.

I poke my head inside the curtain and find Sunny and Paige staring at me like I'm crazy. But Katarina looks surprisingly calm.

"What are we going to do?" Paige asks me.

"What are we going to do?" I ask Katarina.

"Girls, keep your bloomers on!" Katarina says. "You'd be surprised how often this happened in the Middle Ages."

"A play starting late?"

"No, food poisoning. There was no refrigeration, you know. It was a very messy era. Glorious, but messy. The things I could tell you . . ."

I shout, "Katarina, there's no time! What are we going to do?"

"A simple antinausea spell. They'll be as good as new with one stroke of the wand."

I sigh with relief and head for the door.

Two minutes later, we're outside the auditorium, where the kids are still barfing in the bushes. Katarina has told me what to say, so I chant, "Vomit free you shall be!" and toss the spell.

The kids straighten up and turn around. They look a lot less green, and they're not throwing up. . . .

. . . but they still look pretty sick. They collapse to the ground, exhausted.

"Come on, Scott! It's showtime!" I try to pull him to his feet, but he just flops down on the grass and holds his stomach. He says in a low, sick voice, "I'll be fine in a couple of hours."

Katarina looks bewildered. This is not the expression I want to see.

"Why didn't it work?" I ask.

Katarina says, "You didn't have enough magic left to change that many people at once."

"Then let me just change some of them! We can do the play with five or six people!"

"You've already cast the spell. They'll be like this till midnight."

I look over at the kids. They may not be throwing up, but they're not going to be acting or singing or dancing anytime soon.

I feel like screaming. We were so close! I planned for everything but a poisoned protein shake!

To add insult to injury, Seymour the squirrel runs out onto a tree limb and starts chattering at me. I've had all I can take. "Shut up, Seymour!" I shout. "I'm sorry you hate me, but there's nothing I can do about it. Do you hear me? Nothing!"

He just keeps chattering. I'm sure if I could understand squirrel I would be really insulted right now. As he sits on the branch, he looks almost human.

"Hmmmm . . ." I say. "Seymour would make a wonderful prince. What do you think?"

I'm a little surprised when Katarina nods yes. "My thought exactly!"

Sunny is worried. "Wait—you're going to change him into a prince? But he hates you!"

I say, "We talked about it in the bathroom, remember? Katarina said that as long as the spell lasts, the animals forget they're animals and think they're humans."

"I don't have to kiss him, do I?" Paige asks. "I don't want to kiss a squirrel!"

"No, you don't have to kiss him," I say.

Katarina says, "Here's the spell: 'On count of three, Cinderella's prince you shall be.'"

As I fish the wand out of my pocket, Sunny still looks worried. "But he won't know his part!" she says.

Katarina shrugs. "He'll think he's really a prince and that Paige is really Cinderella. It's method acting at its finest."

I point the wand at Seymour and chant, "On count of three, Cinderella's prince you shall be. One, two, three!"

WHUMP!

A handsome prince falls out of the tree and lands at Paige's feet. He looks up at her and says, "Hello, peasant girl. I don't know you, but something in you speaks to my very soul." Paige

looks totally grossed out when he takes her hand and starts kissing it.

Okay, we have a prince! I turn back to Sunny, Paige, and Katarina. "Who else do we absolutely have to have?"

Paige says, "The evil stepmother. And the stepsisters. And the fairy godmother."

I tell Paige and Sunny, "Take him inside. I'll be there in a minute with the rest of the actors."

Not very long after that, I run backstage carrying a cage full of white mice from Mr. Carver's science classroom. Sunny, Katarina, and Paige are peering through the curtain at the impatient audience.

"I'm back!" I say. "Where's the prince?"

Paige points offstage to a storage closet where the prince is turning a light on and off, fascinated. "What's he doing?" I ask.

"He thinks the light is magic," Sunny says. "He won't stop."

"Good!"

I get busy with the wand and turn one of the mice into the tall, thin, evil stepmother, who screeches at Paige to get back to work cleaning. Next, I turn another mouse into the first ugly stepsister, who orders Paige to brush her hair.

Tossing the spell at a third mouse, I say, "On count of three, Cinderella's stepsister you shall be. One, two, three!"

The mouse grows up and up and up into the other stepsister. She's half-human, but she's also half-mouse, with watery pink eyes, white whiskers, and a long, long tail. I know the stepsisters are supposed to be ugly, but she's *ugly*.

I ask Katarina, "What's wrong with her?"

"You're out of magic."

"That can happen?"

"Yes, when you're new. It never happened to me, mind you. But it can happen."

"But I can't be out of magic! We still need a fairy godmother for the play!"

Katarina smiles at me. "I'm looking at one right now!"

I turn, hoping that Chloe Martin has stumbled back in. And then I realize what Katarina's thinking. "No! I can't do it! I'll throw up, and there's already been too much of that!"

On the other side of the curtain, the audience claps and chants, "Start the play! Start the play!"

Yikes.

I go outside and nudge Chloe Martin. "Chloe! Chloe! You've got to go on!" She just groans and turns away. So I take her cloak and wand. Thank goodness I didn't have beanie weenies for dinner.

As I rush back toward the auditorium, I trip over one of the other green-faced kids.

Oh, *crud*! This is why tonight's whole plan won't work. There are a dozen sick kids back here, and every one of them has family members in the audience who will wonder why they're not onstage. I can't exactly make an announcement that they're sick in the parking lot.

What am I going to do?

CHAPTER

32

This is what I do:

The curtain rises, and a dozen green, groggy kids lie in a pile at the back of the stage. Paige, in her "before" costume, sweeps around them and complains, "The other servants are so lazy I have to do all the work!" To my relief, this gets a laugh from the audience. One problem solved!

I push the evil stepfamily out onto the stage, and they instantly surround Paige and demand that she cook and sew and clean. Frankly, it's better dialogue than what Mr. Griffith wrote. Paige sings her first song and manages to wow the audience even with the stepfamily shouting, "Why are you singing? Get to work!"

It's a lot harder to get the stepfamily *off*stage. Sunny, who's doing all the stage-crew work, finally says, "Hark! The king's messenger needs to talk to you in private!"

They fall for it.

I'm shaking in my shoes, but I go out and sing the fairy-godmother song anyway. I don't throw up, but my British accent sucks.

Then Paige walks behind a cupboard dressed in rags and comes out wearing the diamond dress, which sparkles like a million stars. Wow, just wow. I made the dress, and even I can't believe how beautiful it is. The audience applauds and whistles for what seems like forever.

Next comes the ball scene. Paige and Seymour the prince waltz around the stage like . . . like . . . something out of a fairy tale. Her dress catches the light and throws it back into the auditorium, which suddenly seems full of dancing fireflies. I've never heard this many ooohs and aaahs from a crowd.

Katarina, hovering near me, makes the longest ooooooooooh of all, and then says, "Glur! GLURRRRRRRR!" Hypnotized by the sparkling light, she flies out into the auditorium, her butterfly wings spread their widest and most beautiful. People in the audience look up at her and point—a couple of kids even make a grab for her. But she just keeps reaching for the sparkling light. "Glitterrrrrrrrrrrrrr," she says.

I sprint out into the auditorium and say in my best fairy-godmother voice, "No! You cannot make them all sleep for a hundred years! That is another story!" and then ensnare Katarina in my silk cloak. The audience is confused for a moment, but then they applaud, thinking it's all a special effect.

The waltz ends, and Paige runs away, leaving a slipper behind on the stage. Just like he's supposed to, the prince grabs the slipper and runs after her. And then Sunny and I lock him in the storage closet.

So far, so good. It's actually been kind of fun, though Katarina is cranky about almost getting caught in a glitter trap again. When this is all over, I'm going to buy her a pair of sunglasses.

Sunny pulls a rope to change the backdrop from the ballroom to Cinderella's kitchen, and the stepmother and stepsisters look around in a daze. "This is so confusing!" the stepmother finally says. "How did we get back in the kitchen?"

Offstage, I open the storage-closet door and find the prince sitting on the floor talking to the glass slipper. "Where are you, my darling?" he's murmuring.

I point toward the stage. "She's out that way!" He rushes past me so fast he almost knocks me down.

As he runs onto the stage, the stepsisters tackle him and throw him to the ground. The first stepsister shouts, "I've got him! He's mine!" And the second stepsister shouts, "No, *I've* got him!" The girls roll around on the ground clawing at each other, which gives the prince time to crawl away and finally reach Cinderella.

He puts the slipper on Paige's foot and says, "My darling, I have found you! Let the happily-ever-after begin!" He tries to give her a big, sloppy kiss, but Paige manages to slip away from him to sing the big finale. It's a rock version of "I Lost My Shoe" that's been changed into "I *Found* My Shoe and You!"

If I do say so myself, Paige's voice is awesome. She wails, she belts, she trills—in other words, she kicks butt. This is the moment she's been dreaming of. She's the biggest star that our school has ever had.

Paige ends the song on one amazing note that starts low and slowly rises to an impossibly high, perfect sound that hangs in the air like a jewel. We all listen breathlessly, not wanting it to end.

And then she leans up and kisses the prince—I guess she's either forgotten he's a squirrel or she's ignoring it. Either way, it's a moment so beautiful that I almost cry.

I finally remember to motion to Sunny to lower the curtain and end the play. There's complete silence from the audience. I have a split second of fear: did they not like it after all?

But then the entire audience rises to its feet, clapping and cheering and whistling and calling out Paige's name.

Sunny high-fives me. "You did it! You did it!"

Katarina says, "Excuse me; *we* did it!"

Sunny raises the curtain again for the cast members to take their bows. The food-poisoning kids are still in a green heap, and the animal-humans are wandering around the stage aimlessly (the second stepsister is even chewing on her dress like it's dinner). But it doesn't matter, because all eyes are on Paige, standing at center stage and glowing with happiness.

As the roars of approval continue, Paige scans the audience, looking at every single seat. And her happiness drains away like water from a bathtub.

Katarina stiffens. "Uh-oh."

"What, uh-oh?" I say.

"That is not the face of a girl who just had her dream come true."

"Sure it is!"

"Trust me. I've been fairy godmother to six thousand, three hundred and twelve girls, and I know the dream-come-true face. And that's not it."

"But that means . . ." I break out in a cold sweat. I know exactly what that means. It means no dream for Paige, no dream for me, and a lifetime of dryerdom for Katarina. I say, "We've done everything she wanted!"

Suddenly, Mr. Griffith staggers onto the stage, still looking sick. He pushes in front of Paige, who seems perfectly happy to give up the spotlight. She walks into the wings with the prince following her like a puppy and the evil stepfamily close behind.

Mr. Griffith, wiping his mouth with the back of his hand, says to the audience, "Thank you, thank you! I've been near death for the past few hours, but there is no greater balm than the sweet sound of your applause. So I have dragged myself away from the abyss of illness long enough to acknowledge your love. I am glad my little opus has moved and delighted you." He clutches his stomach, about to hurl again, but he manages to control it. He sits down on the edge of the stage near the Mellowtones, who all scoot further back in their chairs. "This evening is such a triumph that I feel compelled to acknowledge all the little people who have helped me along the way. Thank you to my preschool teacher, Miss Petrie, who was the first to see that I had talent. Kudos must also go to my first-grade teacher, Mrs. Stone, who introduced me to the Bard. I had occasional clashes of temperament with my second-grade teacher, Mrs. Brandenberg, but there is no art without conflict. . . ." He drones on and on and on, but the audience is too polite to get up and leave.

Backstage, the prince clings to Paige, all kissy-face, while she simultaneously checks her text messages and tries to push him away. Unfazed, he says, "But, my love! I want to kiss you a thousand times while we plan our wedding!"

I tell him, "Go sit in the corner, and make a list of everyone you want to invite!"

The prince, happy to be given a job, scurries into the corner and starts list-making: "We must invite the Queen of England; Albert of Monaco; Her Majesty, Queen Sirikit of Thailand; Queen Latifah . . ." Not too shabby.

Paige keeps looking at her cell phone unhappily.

"Is everything all right?" I ask.

Instead of answering, she holds up her phone to show me a text: *Delayed with paperwork. Will be home around 10. Dad.*

What a jerk, I think. My dad would have walked over broken glass to see me in this play. But I'm not going to say that out loud.

"What a jerk!" Katarina says. Out loud.

I wince, but Paige says, "It's true. He's a big jerk who doesn't care about me at all. Nothing I do matters to him!" She bursts into tears, and Sunny and I both hug her.

"It's going to be all right," I say.

Katarina shakes her head. "No, it's not. We're doomed. One hundred and ten percent doomed. What a fiasco! I've successfully made dreams come true for six thousand, three hundred and twelve girls. I got the fairy-godmother-of-the-year award for seventy-two years running. Now it's over, done, kaput!" Katarina sits on my shoulder, buries her head in my hair, and sobs.

When Sunny starts crying, too, I know this is the saddest moment of my life. One more second, and I'm going to start bawling myself.

But I don't.

I pull away from the hug. "You guys, stop crying right now. I mean it! Stop crying!"

They look at me through teary eyes.

"We're not giving up yet! There's three hours till midnight. Paige's dream is to have her dad see her in the play. If he won't come to the play, we'll take the play to him."

Katarina says, "We can't do that! You don't have any magic left!"

"We've got Paige. We've got the actors." I point at the prince and the stepfamily. "We've still got the costumes. We can put on the play again at Paige's house."

Sunny asks, "You think that will work?"

"Sure it will!"

Honestly, I'm not sure at all. But it's our only chance.

———

When I go out to the auditorium to talk to Mom and Dad, Mr. Griffith is still sitting on the stage thanking people: "And I can't forget Stacey Sniderman at Camp Entertainus, who gave me the lead in *Annie* despite the controversy, truly proving that the sun will come out tomorrow. Also in that fabulous cast were Nathan Wallace, Alison Chatsworth, Carlos Jimenez, and . . ."

I crawl over a couple of parents who are so bored they're just about sleeping in their chairs and reach Mom. "Lacey! You were wonderful!" she whispers. "You didn't tell us you were going to be *in* the play!"

Dad leans over: "I got it all on my iPhone."

And Madison says, too loudly, "Make that green man stop talking, Lacey!" There are snickers all around and a "You said it!" from a bored-looking guy behind us.

I whisper, "Paige is having a slumber party to celebrate the play. Can I go? Please? Sunny's going."

Dad whispers back, "I'll let you go if you make that man stop talking."

Mom giggles and says, "Sure you can. Don't stay up too late."

Mr. Griffith seems to have finished his speech, and a couple of people start clapping. He gives them a dirty look and continues, "Now, on to the college years!"

Dad groans.

CHAPTER
33

Katarina flutters ahead as Sunny, Paige, and I walk toward Paige's house with the prince and the stepfamily right behind us. The prince is happy just to be near Paige, but the stepmother and stepsisters have been complaining for the past ten minutes: "Where's our carriage!" "Find a peasant and confiscate his horse!" "I hate walking!"

Paige says, "I *love* walking!"

The love-struck prince eagerly bobs his head in agreement. "I love walking, too, dearest!"

The stepsister with the tail hears this and plasters a smile on her face. "I adore walking!" This sets off another round of comments as each of them tries to outdo the others about how she loves walking more than anything in the world.

Katarina can't take any more. "Shut up! One more word out of any of you and I'll turn you into toads!" I know she can't do

it, but they don't. They all shrink away from her and clamp their mouths shut.

So, for a moment it *is* quiet as we walk in the cool, clear night. Then: *ROWF! ROWF! ROWF!* A dog lunges at me from behind a picket fence. It's Barnaby, who seems to have thought about things in the past few days and decided he hates me even more than he did before. *ROWF! ROWF! ROWF!* We pass the house, but the sound of the barking follows us.

Dogs all over the neighborhood start barking, too, as if Barnaby had been warning them that there was a monster named Lacey in town. I don't know what I'm going to do if we don't get Paige her dream come true. I don't want to be treated like a monster by every animal I meet; I really don't.

Sunny seems to know how I'm feeling and squeezes my hand. "Your plan is going to work," she says.

I sure hope so.

It's a quarter past nine when Paige unlocks the door to her house.

The prince tells her, "What a charming hovel you have, my dear. If you like, we can have it moved into the west wing of my castle. *Our* castle."

Katarina snorts, "Castles are overrated."

Feeling like a general commanding her troops, I say, "Everybody, focus! We've only got half an hour until Paige's dad gets home. The living room already has a fireplace, so let's set up there."

Katarina supervises as Sunny, Paige, and I move things around. The prince tries to be helpful but just gets in the way, and the stepfamily doesn't even try. So we move them all into the kitchen and distract them with microwave popcorn. When I pull out the bag, they think I'm a fairy godmother with great powers. Microwave popcorn *is* pretty magical, if you think about it.

By five minutes to ten, we're ready. The furniture has been moved. Paige is in her rags costume and holds a broom, ready to sweep the fireplace. Sunny has found a couple of flashlights to use as spotlights.

And Katarina sits on the couch and shakes her head a lot.

Ten o'clock rolls by.

And then 10:15.

And then 10:30. Where is he?

Around 10:45, Paige gets a text: *Won't be home for a couple more hours. Call Mrs. Folz and ask her to come over.* She angrily throws her phone against the wall.

I don't waste even a second being mad at him. I just say, "Paige, I need to borrow your bike."

CHAPTER
34

When Katarina and I reach the hospital where Paige's father works, it's after eleven. I tell Katarina, "I'm going to make him come home if I have to drag him out by his toes."

"How many times do I have to say it? You don't have any magic left!"

"Not everything in this world depends on magic."

"That's why so many things in this world don't work."

I go in through the sliding glass doors. Katarina zips in after me just as the doors close, narrowly avoiding getting squished flat.

I walk up to the security guard at the front desk. "I need to see one of the doctors. It's urgent."

The guard looks like he's heard this a thousand times before. He drones, "For a medical emergency, go outside and to the left, to the emergency room. Otherwise, please call back tomorrow for an appointment."

"No, it's gotta be tonight!"

"The emergency room is outside and to the left."

"Dr. Harrington's not in the emergency room. He's doing paperwork."

The guard gets a funny look. Is it fear? "No one bothers Dr. Harrington. *No one.*"

"But I have to see him!"

"The last person who bothered him got fired. That's why I have this job. Go home."

"But—"

"Go home!"

He turns back to playing solitaire on his computer. What am I going to do? I can't even get past the security guard!

Suddenly, there's a loud little voice: "The jack of hearts on the queen of clubs."

"Thanks," the guard says, only half paying attention.

"You're welcome," Katarina coos.

The guard looks up and sees her perched on the top of his monitor, flapping her sparkly wings. He looks over at me, panic in his eyes. "Do you see that?"

I instantly understand what Katarina's doing and play along. "See what?" I ask, in my most innocent voice.

He points a shaking finger at Katarina. "That."

I say, "I don't see a thing."

Katarina waves her arms, crosses her eyes, and shouts, "Boo!"

The guard scrambles out of his chair and backs away. She flies into the air and zooms straight at his face with a blood-curdling scream. As he runs toward the sliding doors, I can't resist calling after him: "The emergency room is outside and to the left!"

"Thank you, Katarina," I say after he's gone.

"No chitchat! Where's his office?"

We check the directory and take the elevator up to room number 302. There's a nameplate on the frosted-glass door: DR. STEPHEN HARRINGTON—DIRECTOR OF INTERNAL MEDICINE. Knocking, I say, "Dr. Harrington?"

There's no answer, but through the frosted glass I can see that the lights are on. I knock a little louder. "Dr. Harrington? I need to talk to you!"

There's a gruff voice from inside. "GO AWAY!"

I can see why the guard is so scared of him. But I knock some more and keep calling, "Dr. Harrington! Dr. Harrington!"

"I said, GO AWAY!" The voice is even gruffer and scarier than before.

Katarina flies into my jacket pocket. "I took care of the security guard. You take care of this one." Then she zips the pocket shut.

I knock and knock and knock. Finally, the door bursts open,

and Dr. Harrington comes out, his face red and furious-looking.
"I hope you don't like your job, because—" Then he looks down
and sees that it's me. Or at least, he sees that it's a twelve-year-
old girl and not the nurse he was expecting, because I don't
think he has a clue who I am.

I know I've only got a second or two before he slams the door
in my face, so I just say, "You're a bad father."

"What?"

"You heard me. Paige wanted one thing from you: to see her
in the play. And you missed it." I start pulling him by the hand.

"But it's not too late. We're ready to put on the whole play for you at your house. You just have to come with me."

Dr. Harrington takes his hand back. "Little girl, I don't know what you're talking about, but I don't have time for this."

"You have to make time! I'm talking about Paige, your daughter, the one who's been trying and trying for months just to get you to notice her."

In a quiet voice that's somehow even scarier than the loud one, he says, *"Go away."* And then he steps back into his office and closes the door in my face.

I call, "She's already lost her mother! And now she's lost you, too! It's not right!"

But there's not a word from inside.

CHAPTER

35

A couple of minutes before midnight, I head up the stairs to Paige's front door. Katarina is so depressed that she won't even come out of my pocket.

Ten days ago, I was walking up these same stairs with takeout, and the only thing I was worried about was my ugly lime-green T-shirt. The world was so uncomplicated then. I think about how envious I was of Paige, with her perfect looks and her perfect life. Really, I was the one with the perfect life, if only I'd known it. I'd give anything to have it back.

I open the front door, and it's Crazytown inside. Paige holds the diamond dress over her head, trying to keep it away from the clutching fingers of the ugly stepsisters. They're yelling at the top of their lungs: "Give me the dress!" "I want it!" "No, I want it!"

On the other side of the room, the stepmother has her bony hands around the prince's neck as she shouts: "I don't care which of my daughters you marry! But you're going to marry one of them!"

All he manages to say is a strangled "Nevvverrrrr!!!!"

A chair is shoved under the closed bathroom door, and Sunny yells from inside, "Let me out! Let me out!"

I don't know who to help first, so for a moment, I just watch. In the middle of struggling with the stepsisters, Paige sees me and asks, "Is he coming?"

"No," I say.

With that one awful little word, the fight goes out of Paige, and she lets the diamond dress drop. Each stepsister grabs a sleeve, and they yank it between them, screeching like cats. (Which is odd, because they're mice.) The sisters finally tear the dress in two with a harsh ripping sound that sends a shudder down my spine. Diamonds fly all over the room—so beautiful, but so worthless.

There's another sound that I can't quite place. Like a heart-beat . . . or a distant clock chiming. Katarina pokes her head out of my pocket and wails: "Oh noooooooo!!!! It's midnight! Six thousand, three hundred and twelve girls, and it's all come down to this!"

There's quiet in the room as everyone listens to the clock chime on and on. At the final stroke, there are tiny fizzling sounds like sparklers burning out. The diamonds from the dress vanish into dust.

The stepmother and stepsisters become mice again. And the prince, making one last kissy-face, is transformed back into plain old Seymour the squirrel.

All the animals look around with dazed, blinking eyes. Then their eyes focus on me, and they hate me again. Seymour jumps up on the mantel and chatters angrily.

"What's happening?" Sunny shouts from the bathroom. When I let her out, she looks at the angry animals and instantly understands. Without another word, she gathers up the mice and puts them in the bathtub.

She comes back into the living room and tries to shoo Seymour out the window nearest to the mantel. "Go home to your tree!" she says. He hops onto the windowsill, but then sits glaring at me.

I say, "Let him stay. This is what the rest of my life is going to be like, so I'd better get used to it."

We all slump on the couch. Katarina, too sad to fly, crawls out of my pocket and walks away.

"Where are you going?" I ask.

"Laundry room. There's a dryer with my name on it." And she trudges out of sight.

I feel terrible, because I've made things worse. Before, Paige could tell herself that her father would be there for her if he knew it was important. Now, she doesn't even have that. "I'm so sorry, Paige," I say.

She looks miserable. "It's not your fault that my dad doesn't love me. It's mine."

Seemingly out of nowhere, there's a man's voice: "Don't *ever* say that!"

Paige's father stands in the doorway. She leaps to her feet and runs over to him. "Dad! You're home!"

He hugs her tightly but a little awkwardly, like he's gotten out of practice.

"I'm *so* happy you're home," Paige says.

He looks down and tells her, "I should have been here sooner."

"It's all right," Paige says.

"No, it's not all right." His eyes are shiny with tears. "After your mother died, I thought work would save me. . . . I'm so sorry."

She looks up at him a little uncertainly.

"But I'm here now," he says. "I don't want to be a bad father anymore."

"You're not a bad father!"

"I'm a horrible father! But I promise to do better. Mom's gone, but we're still a family, aren't we?"

She hugs him close, happy tears running down her face. And even with the tears, *this* looks like the face of a girl whose dream has come true.

Then Paige's father says, "I'm told you're putting on a play for me tonight. I want to hear you sing."

Oh, drat! Why couldn't he have come ten minutes ago, when Paige sounded amazing? This is going to ruin everything. I'm not saying he'll stop loving her when he hears her sing. But her voice, as Katarina keeps pointing out, stinks!

So I tell Dr. Harrington, "The cast had to go home. We can't do the play. Too bad! And it's getting really late." I stretch my arms out wide and pretend to yawn. "Wow, I'm tired."

I elbow Sunny, and she stretches and yawns, too. "Bedtime for us! Come on, Paige!"

Dr. Harrington says, "Just one song. Please, Paige. For me?"

Double drat. Paige can't say no to this. He said, *Please.*

So Paige opens her mouth and sings, *"I lost my shoe and you . . ."*

She sounds every bit as awful as I remember, maybe even worse. Katarina flies out of the laundry room and hovers next to me with her fingers in her ears.

Paige sings, *"I can't believe it's true. I don't know what to do. I'm feeling so very bluuuuuuuuuuue."*

The musical torture finally ends, and there's a long pause as Paige's father looks at her. My guess is that he's just decided to put her up for adoption and rent her room to some other kid. I'm the worst fairy godmother ever.

But then he smiles. He tells Paige, "You sing just like your mother. I always loved the way she sang." He hugs her like he's never going to let her go.

Sunny blurts out, "But she sounds *terrible!*"

Katarina nods in agreement and flits out of sight.

"Not to me." Dr. Harrington beams.

There's a clattering from the windowsill. It's Seymour again, staring right at me. Oh, geez. He's got an acorn in his paws. Let me guess—he's gonna throw it at me. But he keeps looking at me and holding out the acorn like it's a . . . like it's a . . .

Like it's a present?

I hesitantly walk over to the window, and he holds up the acorn as high as he can. I take it from him, and he nods and chatters and nuzzles against me.

Dr. Harrington says, "I've never seen a squirrel do that before!"

This is weird. Because Seymour seems to like me again. But that can't be right, can it? I say, "Excuse me. I have to use the bathroom."

As I walk away, Dr. Harrington says to Paige, "Sing me another song from the play!"

Sunny says, a little too loudly, "I have to go to the bathroom, too!" and runs after me.

We reach the bathroom and shut the door behind us. Katarina is already perched on the edge of the bathtub, where the mice are. "Grab one."

I hesitantly reach down and pick up a mouse. Instead of scratching and squirming like before, it snuggles in my hand.

I excitedly pick up the other mice, and they blink at me

happily with their round pink eyes. They don't hate me! In fact, they like me!

Sunny asks, "What happened? It's past midnight! I'm *confused*!"

Katarina looks every bit as confused as Sunny does. Then she looks out the bathroom window and sees the big, round, full moon. She smiles with sudden understanding and turns back to me and Sunny with an "I've known it all along" look.

She says, "I've successfully made dreams come true for six thousand, three hundred and twelve girls. And I've always done it before midnight on the night of the full moon. That's because I'm so organized and talented. What you girls forget is that on the last day it's not the midnight, it's the full moon that counts. Deep down, Paige's dream wasn't to be Cinderella in the play, it was for her father to notice her again. And I accomplished that! I now have an unbroken record of six thousand, three hundred and thirteen girls!" Then she stops herself and tells me, "No, *we* accomplished it. Credit where credit is due." She says, "Sunny, you helped, too. But your hair is *terrible*!"

Sunny looks hurt and hides her bangs with her hands.

Katarina says, "Lacey? I want my wand back."

Wow, she doesn't waste any time. I pull the little wand out of my pocket and give it to her.

She taps the wand cautiously. "Since the assignment is over, the wand should have re-bonded to me."

Katarina squeezes her eyes shut and clutches the wand close to her with both hands. I know exactly what she's thinking: *Oh please, oh please, oh please, oh please,* oh please.

Katarina finally raises the wand over her head and says, "Bangs horrific, turn terrific!" And with a single stroke of the wand, Sunny's butchered hair grows out luxuriantly.

Katarina happily kisses the wand and shouts, "Katarina Sycorax is back in business!"

Sunny runs her hands through her long, beautiful hair. "Thank you so much!"

"You're very welcome. I don't know what idiot let you get your bangs cut like that."

"But the hair will only last till midnight, right?" I say.

"Yes, but by then I'll be gone and won't have to look at her anymore."

Sunny thinks about it and says, "Well, better than nothing!" She's definitely a glass-is-half-full kind of girl.

CHAPTER

36

After all the excitement, I think Paige, Sunny, and I will never get to sleep, but we conk out the second our heads hit the pillows (sleeping bags, actually, but we're so tired they feel like pillows to us).

In the morning, I wake up *and smell smoke*! I reach over and shake Sunny and Paige awake, shouting, "The house is on fire!"

But we find out it's not a fire—it's Paige's father, cooking pancakes for us in the kitchen. And even though they're burned on the outside and raw in the middle, we tell him they're great.

And we're not even lying. They're great because Paige's dad is here, and he's making them. He burned them with love. And love is all you need.

Well, love and a lot of syrup.

I look at Paige's happy face, and I'm proud to have been a fairy godmother, even if it was only for a couple of weeks.

Speaking of fairy godmothers . . . where's Katarina?

Hurrying back into Paige's bedroom, I call, "Katarina? Katarina?" She's not there. Then I notice a tiny note pinned to my sleeping bag. I must have missed it when I thought the house was on fire.

I pick up the note and read:

Off to my new assignment! No more glitter traps, okay!
Katarina.

Wow. Not very sentimental, is she?

I walk home, feeling a little sad. I can't believe I'm saying this, but I'm going to miss Katarina. On the bright side, the pigeons aren't pooping on my head.

When I go by Barnaby's fence, there's a loud *ROWF! ROWF! ROWF!* The old basset hound comes barreling down off the porch, and instead of stopping at the fence he leaps right over it and knocks me down. Geez! Does he still hate me?

No. He loooooooooooooves me. He wags his tail and covers my entire face with doggy drool. I laugh and try to push him away, saying, "Barnaby! Stop!" But he's not going anywhere.

"Do you need some help?" a voice says.

Oh no.

Oh no!

OH NO!

It's Scott Dearden, who somehow rode up on his bike without my seeing him. And I'm lying on the sidewalk covered in dog spit! I wish I still had the magic wand, so I could make myself disappear.

As Scott takes Barnaby by the collar and puts him in the yard, I stumble to my feet and try to wipe myself off.

Scott turns back to me with this strange, almost nervous expression on his face. I must look really scary. I mean, *really* scary.

He stammers, "There's a home game at the high school next Friday. Do you want to go with me?"

Inside my head, I'm happy-shrieking louder than Ann Estey and Madison put together. But I manage to say, "Okay."

Scott smiles. "Great! See you Friday!" He gets back on his bike and pedals away.

When he disappears around the corner, I lie back down on the sidewalk until the shrieking in my head goes away.

It takes a long, long time.

The first thing I see when I get home is Julius napping on the window seat. He wakes up and meows at me. I give him a hug so big that it's almost the Heimlich maneuver for cats, but he doesn't seem to mind. In fact, he purrs louder than I've ever heard him purr.

In the kitchen, Mom, Dad, and Madison are squeezing homemade pasta out of the pasta machine. They all smile when they see me. Dad says, "Hi, Lacey! I hope you're in a linguine mood!"

"It's linguinepalooza!" Madison tries to say, but she ends up mushing it into *lingipooz*.

I know what she means and tell her, "Yum!"

I go into my room to change clothes. When I put Julius down on the bed, he stretches out and is instantly sound asleep.

Then I hear a little voice: "Sorry I vanished like that."

Katarina flies in the window, her butterfly wings catching the sunlight. She says, "I wanted to come back and say good-bye. In a couple hundred years, you might make a decent fairy godmother."

I guess that's the highest praise I'll ever get from Katarina. I say, "Thanks. But I'll leave the fairy-godmothering to you."

"Smart girl!"

"Will I ever see you again?"

"You never know. Gotta go! Duty calls!"

"'Bye, Katarina!"

"Good-bye, Lacey."

She turns away from me and floats into the air with a few beats of her wings, so pretty in the sunlight she takes my breath away.

And then . . .

WHOOSH! Julius leaps into the air to eat her again.

ZAP! Katarina blasts him with her wand, and he turns into an orange toad, too small to eat even a fairy. The Julius-toad meows at me plaintively.

I pick him up. "You kind of had that coming, Julius. And it's just till midnight."

Katarina smiles at me. Is that really a tear in her eye? She says, "If you tell a living soul I said this, I'll deny it. But you did good, Lacey."

And with a flutter of wings, she's gone.

CHAPTER
37

On Monday morning, Sunny and I walk to school together. Along the way, we stop at Paige's house, but she's already left.

Sunny's shoulders slump. "She said she was going to wait for us."

I have a sinking feeling, too. What if Paige doesn't want to be seen with us anymore? Cheerleaders don't mix with normal kids. It's sad, but it's just the way middle school works.

As Sunny and I push our way down the crowded school hallway, Sunny sees Paige first. She points. "There she is!"

Paige has her back to us, and is taping a giant poster to the wall.

"Hey, Paige! Paige!" Sunny calls.

Paige doesn't turn around. It's worse than I thought—she's not even talking to us.

I pull Sunny in the other direction. We don't need this kind of humiliation.

Then Paige shouts, "Lacey! Wait!"

I look back. Paige, a big smile on her face, steps away from the poster and points.

OMG!

In the glitteriest glitter I've ever seen, the poster says, CONGRATULATIONS, LACEY! OUR NEW ZOO INTERN!

I read it three times. Zoo intern? Zoo intern? *Zoo intern!*

Paige runs up to us, and we all jump up and down, screaming. I shout, "I'm the new zoo intern! I'm the new zoo intern!" I'm louder than Madison. I'm louder than Ann Estey. I'm LOUD.

After a lot more jumping and screaming, I ask Paige, "How did you know I got the internship?"

"Principal Nazarino texted me first thing this morning and asked me to make a poster. How do you like it?"

Hiding my smile, I pretend to squint at it. Then I say, "Needs more glitter."

ACKNOWLEDGMENTS

Lacey Unger-Ware's first book has many godmothers and godfathers. These include Joseph Veltre, Bayard Maybank, Devra Lieb, and Bob Hohman; Michael Schenkman and Cuffe B. Owens; Tom Brauner, Melonia Musser-Brauner, and Dash Musser-Brauner; Laurie Mattson, Tom Mattson, Lauren Mattson, Matt Mattson, Josh Capps, Maelena Mattson, Michelle Hardy, Breezie Daniel, and Daniel Wake; and Lisa Holmes, John Biondo, Gerardo Paron, and Becky Bristow.

We also want to thank our wonderful editor, Catherine Onder—who waves her wand and makes us write better—as well as Hayley Wagreich and everyone else at Disney-Hyperion.

And special thanks to our first and most constant reader, Laura Hopper.